All About My Naughty Little Sister

DOROTHY EDWARDS

All About My Naughty Little Sister

illustrated by SHIRLEY HUGHES

METHUEN CHILDREN'S BOOKS

LONDON

All these stories first appeared in:

MY NAUGHTY LITTLE SISTER © 1952 *by Dorothy Edwards*

MORE NAUGHTY LITTLE SISTER STORIES

AND SOME OTHERS © 1957 *by Dorothy Edwards*

MY NAUGHTY LITTLE SISTER'S FRIENDS

© 1962 *by Dorothy Edwards*

This edition first published 1969 by Methuen & Co Ltd
Illustrations © 1969 by Shirley Hughes
Reprinted 1971, 1973 and 1975
Printed in Great Britain by
Fletcher & Son Ltd, Norwich

ISBN 0 416 10830 X

Contents

5

Foreword

A LONG TIME ago when I was a little girl, I had a sister who was littler than me. My little sister had brown eyes, and red hair, and a pinkish nose, and she was very, very stubborn.

When you told her to smile for her photograph, she said, "No, I don't want to," but if you gave her an ice-cream, or a chocolate biscuit, or a toffee-drop, she said "Thank you," and smiled and smiled.

So you must try to imagine her with a chocolate biscuit *and* an ice-cream *and* a toffee-drop, so that you can see her at her very, very best. . . .

Imagine very hard. . . . There, doesn't she look a bright, happy child?

Well now, I'm going to tell you some stories about her which I think you will like.

DOROTHY EDWARDS

I · The very first story

A VERY LONG time ago, when I was a little girl, I didn't have a naughty little sister at all. I was a child all on my own. I had a father and a mother, of course, but I hadn't any other little brothers or sisters – I was quite alone.

I was a very lucky little girl because I had a dear granny and a dear grandad and lots of kind aunts and uncles to make a fuss of me. They played games with me, and gave me toys and took me for walks, and bought me ice-creams and told me stories, but I hadn't got a little sister.

Well now, one day, when I was a child on my own, I went to stay with my kind godmother-aunt in the country. My kind godmother-aunt was very good to me. She took me out every day to see the farm animals and to pick flowers, and she read stories to me, and let me cook little cakes and jam tarts in her oven, and I was very, very happy. I didn't want to go home one bit.

Then, one day, my godmother-aunt said, "Here is a letter from your father, and what do you think he says?"

My aunt was smiling and smiling.

"What do you think he says?" she asked. "He says that

you have a little baby sister waiting for you at home!"

I *was* excited! I said, "I think I had better go home at once, don't you?" and my kind godmother-aunt said, "I think you had indeed." And she took me home that very day!

My aunt took me on a train and a bus and another bus, and then I was home!

And, do you know, before I'd even got indoors, I heard a waily-waily noise coming from the house, and my godmother-aunt said, "That is your new sister."

"Waah-waah," my little sister was saying, "waah-waah."

I was surprised to think that such a very new child could make so much noise, and I ran straight indoors and straight upstairs and straight into my mother's bedroom. And there was my good kind mother sitting up in bed smiling and smiling, and there, in a cot that used to be my old cot, was my new cross little sister crying and crying!

My mother said, "Sh-sh, baby, here is your big sister come to see you." My mother lifted my naughty little baby sister out of the cot, and my little sister stopped crying at once.

My mother said, "Come and look."

My little sister was wrapped up in a big, woolly, white shawl, and my mother undid the shawl and there was my little sister! When my mother put her down on the bed, my little sister began to cry again.

She was a little, little red baby, crying and crying.

"Waah-waah, waah-waah" – like that. Isn't it a nasty noise?

My little sister had tiny hands and tiny little feet. She went on crying and crying, and curling up her toes, and beating with her arms in a very cross way.

My mother said, "She likes being lifted up and cuddled. She is a very good baby when she is being cuddled and fussed, but when I put her down she cries and cries. She is an artful pussy," my mother said.

I was very sorry to see my little sister crying, and I was disappointed because I didn't want a crying little sister very much, but I went and looked at her. I looked at her little red face and her little screwed up eyes and her little crying mouth and then I said, "Don't cry, baby, don't cry, baby."

And, do you know, when I said, "Don't cry, baby," my little sister *stopped crying*, really stopped crying at once. For me! Because *I* told her to. She opened her eyes and she looked and looked and she didn't cry any more.

My mother said, "Just fancy! She must know you are her own big sister! She has stopped crying."

I was pleased to think that my little sister had stopped crying because she knew I was her big sister, and I put my finger on my sister's tiny, tiny hand and my little sister caught hold of my finger tight with her little curly fingers.

My mother said I could hold my little sister on my lap if I was careful. So I sat down on a chair, and my god-mother-aunt put my little sister on to my lap, and I held her very carefully; and my little sister didn't cry at all. She went to sleep like a good baby.

And do you know, she was so small and so sweet and she held my finger so tightly with her curly little fingers that I loved her and loved her, and although she often cried after that I never minded it a bit, because I knew how nice and cuddly she could be when she was good!

2 · The naughtiest story of all

THIS IS SUCH a very terrible story about my naughty little sister that I hardly know how to tell it to you. It is all about one Christmas-time.

Now, my naughty little sister was very pleased when Christmas began to draw near, because she liked all the excitement of the plum-puddings and the turkeys, and the crackers and the holly, and all the Christmassy-looking shops, but there was one very awful thing about her – she didn't like to think about Father Christmas at all – she said he was a *horrid old man*!

There – I knew you would be shocked at that. But she did. And she said she wouldn't put up her stocking for him.

My mother told my naughty little sister what a good old man Father Christmas was, and how he brought the toys along on Christmas Eve, but my naughty little sister said, "I don't care. And I don't want that nasty old man coming to our house."

Well now, that was bad enough, wasn't it? But the really dreadful thing happened later on.

This is the dreadful thing: one day, my school-teacher

said that a Father Christmas Man would be coming to the school to bring presents for all the children, and my teacher said that the Father Christmas Man would have toys for all our little brothers and sisters as well, if they cared to come along for them. She said that there would be a real Christmas-tree with candles on it, and sweeties and cups of tea and biscuits for our mothers.

Wasn't that a nice thought? Well now, when I told my little sister about the Christmas-tree, she said, "Oh, nice!"

And when I told her about the sweeties she said, "Very, very nice!" But when I told her about the Father Christmas Man, she said, "Don't want *him*, nasty old man."

Still, my mother said, "You can't go to the Christmas-tree without seeing him, so if you don't want to see him all that much, you will have to stay at home."

But my naughty little sister did want to go, very much, so she said, "I will go, and when the horrid Father Christmas Man comes in, I will close my eyes."

So, we all went to the Christmas-tree together, my mother, and I, and my naughty little sister.

When we got to the school, my naughty little sister was very pleased to see all the pretty paperchains that we had made in school hanging all round the classrooms, and when she saw all the little lanterns, and the holly and all the robin-redbreast drawings pinned on the blackboards she smiled and smiled. She was very smily at first.

All the mothers, and the little brothers and sisters who

15

were too young for school, sat down in chairs and desks, and all the big school children acted a play for them.

My little sister was very excited to see all the children dressed up as fairies and robins and elves and Bo-peeps and

things, and she clapped her hands very hard, like all the grown-ups did, to show that she was enjoying herself. And she still smiled.

Then, when some of the teachers came round with bags of sweets, tied up in pretty coloured paper, my little sister smiled even more, and she sang too when all the children sang. She sang, "Away in a manger," because she knew the words very well. When she didn't know the words of some of the singing, she "la-la'd."

After all the singing, the teachers put out the lights, and took away a big screen from a corner of the room, and there was the Christmas-tree, all lit up with candles and shining with silvery stuff, and little shiny coloured balls. There were lots of toys on the tree, and all the children cheered and clapped.

Then the teachers put the lights on again, and blew out the candles, so that we could all go and look at the tree. My little sister went too. She looked at the tree, and she looked at the toys, and she saw a specially nice doll with a blue dress on, and she said, "For me."

My mother said, "You must wait and see what you are given."

Then the teachers called out, "Back to your seats, everyone, we have a visitor coming." So all the children went back to their seats, and sat still and waited and listened.

And, as we waited and listened, we heard a tinkle-tinkle bell noise, and then the schoolroom door opened, and in walked the Father Christmas Man. My naughty little sister had forgotten all about him, so she hadn't time to close her eyes before he walked in. However, when she saw him, my little sister stopped smiling and began to be stubborn.

The Father Christmas Man was very nice. He said he

hoped we were having a good time, and we all said, "Yes," except my naughty little sister – she didn't say a thing.

Then he said, "Now, one at a time, children; and I will give each one of you a toy."

So, first of all each schoolchild went up for a toy, and my naughty little sister still didn't shut her eyes because she wanted to see who was going to have the specially nice doll in the blue dress. But none of the schoolchildren had it.

Then Father Christmas began to call the little brothers and sisters up for presents, and, as he didn't know their names, he just said, "Come along, sonny," if it were a boy, and "come along, girlie," if it were a girl. The Father Christmas Man let the little brothers and sisters choose their own toys off the tree.

When my naughty little sister saw this, she was so worried about the specially nice doll, that she thought that she would just go up and get it.

She said, "I don't like that horrid old beardy man, but I do like that nice doll."

So, my naughty little sister got up without being asked to, and she went right out to the front where the Father Christmas Man was standing, and she said, "That doll, please," and pointed to the doll she wanted.

The Father Christmas Man laughed and all the teachers laughed, and the other mothers and the schoolchildren, and all the little brothers and sisters. My mother did not

laugh because she was so shocked to see my naughty little sister going out without being asked to.

The Father Christmas Man took the specially nice doll off the tree, and he handed it to my naughty little sister and he said, "Well now, I hear you don't like me very much, but won't you just shake hands?" and my naughty little sister said, "No." But she took the doll all the same.

The Father Christmas Man put out his nice old hand for her to shake and be friends, and do you know what that naughty bad girl did? *She bit his hand.* She really and truly did. Can you think of anything more dreadful and terrible? She bit Father Christmas's good old hand, and then she turned and ran and ran out of the school with all the children staring after her, and her doll held very tight in her arms.

The Father Christmas Man was very nice. He said it wasn't a hard bite, only a frightened one, and he made all the children sing songs together.

When my naughty little sister was brought back by my mother, she said she was very sorry, and the Father Christmas Man said, "That's all right, old lady," and because he was so smily and nice to her, my funny little sister went right up to him, and gave him a big "sorry" kiss, which pleased him very much.

And she hung her stocking up after all, and that kind man remembered to fill it for her.

My little sister kept the specially nice doll until she was

quite grown-up. She called it Rosy-primrose, and although she was sometimes bad-tempered with it, she really loved it very much indeed.

3 · My naughty little sister and the book-little-boy

DO YOU LIKE having stories read to you? When I was a little girl I used to like it very much. My little sister liked it too, but she pretended that she didn't.

When my sister and I were very little children we had a kind aunt who used to come and read stories to us. She used to read all the stories that she'd had read to her when *she* was a little girl.

I used to listen and listen and say, "Go on! Go on!" whenever my auntie stopped for a minute, but my little sister used to pretend that she wasn't listening. Wasn't she silly? She used to fidget with her old doll, Rosy-primrose, and pretend that she was playing babies with her, but really she listened and listened too, and heard every word.

Do you know how I knew that she listened and listened? I'll tell you. When my little sister was in bed at night she used to tell the stories all over again to Rosy-primrose.

One day when my aunt came to read to us, she said, "I've got a book here that I won as a Sunday School prize.

I used to like these stories when I was a child. I hope you will like them too."

So our aunt read us a story about a poor little boy. It was a very sad story in the beginning because this poor little boy was very ragged and hungry. It said that he had no breakfast and no dinner and no supper, but it was lovely at the end because a nice, kind lady took him home with her and said she was his real mother and gave him lots of nice things to eat and lots of nice clothes to wear, and a white pony. But the "nothing to eat" part was very sad.

Now, you know, my little sister liked eating, and she was so surprised to hear about the book-little-boy with nothing to eat that she forgot to pretend that she wasn't listening, and she said, "No breakfast?" She said "No breakfast?" in a very little voice.

Our auntie said, "No, no breakfast."

My little sister said, "No dinner?" She said that in a little voice too, because she thought no dinner and no breakfast was terrible.

My aunt said, "No dinner, *and* no supper," and she was so pleased to think that my funny little sister *had* been listening that she said, "Would you like to see the picture?" And my little sister said "please" and I said "please" too.

So our kind aunt showed us the picture in the book that went with the poor little boy story. It was a very miserable picture because the little boy was sitting all alone in the

23

corner of a room, looking very sad. There was an empty plate on the floor beside this poor little boy, and under the picture it said, "*Nothing to eat.*"

Wasn't that sad?

My little sister thought it was very sad. She looked and looked at the picture and she said, "*No* breakfast, *no* dinner, and *no supper*." Like that, over and over again.

My aunt said, "Cheer up. He had lots to eat when his

kind, rich mother took him home in the end; he had a pony too, remember," my aunt said.

But my sister said, "No *picture* dinner. Poor, poor boy," she said.

Well now, when the reading time was over my little sister was a very quiet child. She was very quiet when she had her supper. She sat by the fire and my mother gave her a big piece of buttery bread and a big mug of warm sweet milk, but she was very quiet; she said "thank you" in a tiny quiet voice, and she drank up her milk like a good child. When my mother came to say that the hot-water-bottle was in her bed, she said her prayers in a good quiet way and went straight upstairs.

My mother kissed my warm little sister and said "good night" to her, and my little sister said "good night". But when my kind aunt kissed her and said "good night" to her, my little sister said, "*No* breakfast, *no* dinner," and my auntie said, "No supper," but my little sister smiled and said, "*Yes, supper.*" My little sister looked very smily and pleased with herself.

Wasn't that a funny thing to say, "*No* breakfast, *no* dinner and *Yes, supper?*" My aunt thought it was funny, and so did my mother. They said, "What a funny child you are."

But when our aunt went to go home, and looked for the Sunday School prize-book, she knew why my little sister had said such a funny thing.

Do you know what that silly child had done? She had put her piece of buttery bread inside the Sunday School prize-book, on top of the little book boy's picture. She had given her supper to the book-little-boy!

Of course the book was very greasy and crumby after that, which was a pity because our aunt had kept it very tidy indeed as it had been a prize. I suppose it was a very naughty thing to have done.

But my little sister hadn't *meant* to be naughty. She thought that she had given the book-little-boy her own supper, and you know she was quite a greedy child, so it was a kind thing to do really.

Now you know why she said, "*No* breakfast, *no* dinner, and *Yes, supper*," don't you?

4 · When my father minded my naughty little sister

MY NAUGHTY LITTLE sister had a very cross friend. My little sister's cross friend was called Mr Blakey, and he was a very grumbly old man.

My little sister's friend Mr Blakey was the shoe-mender man, and he had a funny little shop with bits of leather all over the floor, and boxes of nails, and boot-polish, and shoe-laces, all over the place. Mr Blakey had a picture in his shop too. It was a very beautiful picture of a little dog with boots on all four feet, walking in the rain. My little sister loved that picture very much, but she loved Mr Blakey better than that.

Every time we went in Mr Blakey's shop with our mother, my naughty little sister would start meddling with things, and Mr Blakey would say, "Leave that be, you varmint," in a very loud, cross voice, and my little sister would stop meddling at once, just like an obedient child, because Mr Blakey was her favourite man; and one day, when we went into his shop, do you know what she did?

27

She went straight behind the counter and kissed him without being asked. Mr Blakey was very surprised because he had a lot of nails in his mouth, but after that, he always gave her a peppermint humbug after he had shouted at her.

Well, that's about Mr Blakey, in case you wonder who he was later on. Now this is the real story.

One day, my mother had to go out shopping, so she asked my father if he would mind my naughty little sister for the day. My mother said she would take me shopping because I was a big girl, but my little sister was too draggy and moany to go to the big shops.

My father said he would mind my little sister, but my little sister said, "I want to go, I want to go." You know how she said that by now, I think. "I want to go" – like that. And she kicked and screamed.

My mother said, "Oh, dear, how tiresome you are," to my little sister, but my father said, "You'll jolly well do as you're told, old lady."

Then my naughty little sister wouldn't eat her breakfast, but my mother went off shopping with me just the same, and when we had gone, my father looked very fierce, and he said, "What about that breakfast?"

So my naughty little sister ate all her breakfast up, every bit, and she said, "More milk, please," and "more bread, please", so much that my father got tired getting it for her.

Then, as it was a hot day, my father said, "I'll bring my work into the garden, and give an eye to you at the same time."

So my father took a chair and a table out into the garden, and my little sister went out into the garden too, and because my father was there she played good child's games. She didn't tread on the baby seedlings, or pick the flowers, or steal the blackcurrants, or do anything at all wicked. She didn't want my father to look fierce again, and my father said she was a good, nice child.

My little sister just sat on the lawn and played with Rosy-primrose, and she made a tea-party with leaves and nasturtium seeds, and when she wanted something she asked my father for it nicely, not going off and finding it for herself at all.

She said, "Please, Father, would you get me Rosy-primrose's box?" and my father put down his pen, and his writing paper, and got out of his chair, and went and got Rosy-primrose's box, which was on the top shelf of the toy-cupboard and had all Rosy-primrose's tatty old clothes in it.

Then my father did writing again, and then my little sister said, "Please can I have a drink of water?" She said it nicely, "Please," she said.

That was very good of her to ask, because sometimes she used to drink germy water out of the water-butt; but Father wasn't pleased at all, he said, "Bother!" because

he was being a busy man, and he stamped and stamped to the kitchen to get the water for my polite little sister.

But my father didn't know about Rosy-primrose's water. You see, when my little sister had a drink she always gave Rosy-primrose a drink too in a blue doll's cup. So when my father brought back the water, my little sister said, "Where is Rosy-primrose's water?" and my cross father said, "Bother Rosy-primrose," like that, cross and grumbly.

And my father was crosser and grumblier when my little sister asked him to put Rosy-primrose's box back in the toy-cupboard. He said, "That wretched doll again?" and he took Rosy-primrose and shut her in the box too, and put it on top of the bookcase, to show how firm he was going to be. So then my little sister stopped being good.

She started to yell and stamp, and make such a noise that people going by looked over the hedge to see what the matter was. Wouldn't you have been ashamed if it were you stamping and yelling with people looking at you? My naughty little sister wasn't ashamed. *She* didn't care about the people at all; she was a stubborn bad child.

My father was a stubborn man too. He took his table and his chair and his writing things indoors, and shut himself away in his study.

"You'll jolly well stay there till you behave," he said to my naughty little sister.

My naughty little sister cried and cried until my father looked out of the window and said, "Any more of that, and off to bed you go." Then she was quiet, because she didn't want to go to bed.

She only peeped in once after that, but my father said, "Go away, do," and went on writing and writing, and he was so interested in his writing, he forgot all about my little sister, and it wasn't until he began to get hungry that he remembered her at all.

Then my father went out into the kitchen, and there was a lot of nice salad-stuff in the kitchen that our mother had left for lunch. There was junket, too, and stewed pears, and biscuits for my father's and my little sister's lunches. My father remembered my little sister then, and he went to call her for lunch, because it was quite late. It was so late it was four o'clock.

But my little sister wasn't in the garden. My father looked and looked. He looked among the marrows, and behind the runner-bean rows, and under the hedge. He looked in the shed and down the cellar-hole, but there was no little girl.

Then my father went indoors again and looked all over

the house, and all the time he was calling and calling, but there was still no little girl at all.

Then my father got worried. He didn't stop to change his slippers or eat his lunch. He went straight out of the gate, and down the road to look for my little sister. But he couldn't see her at all. He asked people, "Have you seen a little girl with red hair?" and people said, "No."

My father was just coming up the road again, looking so hot and so worried, when my mother and I got off the bus. When my mother saw him, she said, "He's lost that child," because she knows my father and my little sister rather well.

When we got indoors my mother said, "Why haven't you eaten your lunch?" and then my father told her all about the writing, and my bad sister. So my mother said, "Well, if she's anywhere, she's near food of some kind. Have you looked in the larder?" My father said he had. So mother said, "Well, I don't know——"

Then I said something clever. I said, "I expect she is with old Mr Blakey." So we went off to Mr Blakey's shop, and there she was. Fast asleep on a pile of leather bits.

Mr Blakey seemed quite cross with us for having lost her, and my naughty little sister was very cross when we took her away because she said she had had a lovely time with Mr Blakey. Mr Blakey had boiled her an egg in his tea-kettle, and given her some bread and cheese out of news-paper, and let her cut it for herself with one of his nice leathery knives. Mother was cross because she had been looking forward to a nice cup of tea after the bus journey,

and I was cross because my little sister had had such a fine time in Mr Blakey's shop.

The only happy one was my father. He said, "Thank goodness I can work again without having to concentrate on a disagreeable baby." However, that made my little sister cry again, so he wasn't happy for long.

5 · The cross photograph

A LONG TIME ago, our mother made my naughty little sister and me a beautiful coat each.

They were lovely red coats with black buttons to do them up with and curly-curly black fur on them to keep us warm. We were very proud children when we put our new red coats on.

Our mother was proud too, because she had never made any coats before, and she said, "I know! You shall have your photographs taken. Then we can always remember how smart they look."

So our proud mother took my naughty little sister and me to have our photographs taken in our smart red coats.

The man in the photographer's shop was very smart too. He had curly-curly black hair *just* like the fur on our new coats, and he had a pink flower in his buttonhole and a yellow handkerchief that he waved and waved when he took our photographs.

There were lots of pictures in the shop. There were pictures of children, and ladies being married, and ladies smiling, and gentlemen smiling, and pussy-cats with long

fur, and black-and-white rabbits. All those pictures! And
the smart curly-curly man had taken every one himself!

He said we could go and look at his pictures while he

talked to our mother, so I went round and looked at them.
But do you know, my naughty little sister wouldn't look.
She stood still as still and quiet as quiet, and she shut her
eyes.

Yes, she did. She shut her eyes and wouldn't look at
anything. She was being a stubborn girl, and when the

photographer-man said, "Are you both ready?" my bad little sister kept her eyes shut and said, "*No*."

Our mother said, "But surely you want your photograph taken?"

But my naughty little sister kept her eyes shut tight as tight, and said, "No taken! No taken!" And she got so cross, and shouted so much, that the curly man said, "All right then. I will just take your big sister by herself."

"I will take a nice photograph of your big sister," said the photographer-man, "and she will be able to show it to all her friends. Wouldn't you like a photograph of yourself to show to your friends?"

My naughty little sister did want a photograph of herself to show to her friends, but she would not say so. She just said, "No photograph!"

So our mother said, "Oh well, it looks as if it will be only one picture then, for we can't keep this gentleman waiting all day."

So the photographer-man made me stand on a box-thing. There was a little table on the box-thing, and I had to put my hand on the little table and stand up straight and smile.

There was a beautiful picture of a garden on the wall behind me. It was such a big picture that when the photograph was taken it looked just as if I was standing in a real garden. Wasn't that a clever idea?

When I was standing quite straight and quite smily, the

curly photographer-man shone a lot of bright lights, and then he got his big black camera-on-legs and said, "Watch for the dickey-bird!" And he waved and waved his yellow handkerchief. And then "Click!" said the camera, and my picture was safe inside it.

"That's all," said the man, and he helped me to get down.

Now, what do you think? While the man was taking my picture, my little sister had opened her eyes to peep, and when she saw me standing all straight and smily in my beautiful new coat, and heard the man say, "Watch for the dickey-bird," and saw him wave his yellow handkerchief, she stared and stared.

The man said, "That was all right, wasn't it?" and I said, "Yes, thank you."

Then the curly man looked at my little sister and he saw that her eyes weren't shut any more so he said, "Are you going to change your mind now?"

And what do you think? My little sister changed her mind. She stopped being stubborn. She changed her mind and said, "Yes, please," like a good polite child. You see, she hadn't known anything about photographs before, and she had been frightened, but when she saw me having my picture taken, and had seen how easy it was, she hadn't been frightened any more.

She let the man lift her on to the box-thing. She was so small though, that he took the table away and found a little chair for her to sit on, and gave her a teddy-bear to hold.

Then he said, "Smile nicely now," and my naughty little sister smiled very beautifully indeed.

The man said, "Watch for the dickey-bird," and he waved his yellow handkerchief to her, and "click", my naughty little sister's photograph had been taken too!

But what do you think? She hadn't kept smiling. When the photographs came home for us to look at, there was my

little sister holding the teddy-bear and looking as cross as cross.

Our mother *was* surprised; she said, "I thought the man told you to *smile*!"

And what do you think that funny girl said? She said, "I did smile, but there wasn't any dickey-bird, so I stopped."

My mother said, "Oh dear! We shall have to have it taken all over again!"

But our father said, "No, I like this one. It is such a natural picture. I like it as it is." And he laughed and laughed and laughed and laughed.

My little sister liked the cross picture very much too, and sometimes, when she hadn't anything else to do, she climbed up to the looking-glass and made cross faces at herself. *Just* like the cross face in the photograph!

6 · My naughty little sister and the big girl's bed

A LONG TIME ago, my naughty little sister had a nice cot with pull-up sides so that she couldn't fall out and bump herself.

My little sister's cot was a very pretty one. It was pink, and had pictures of fairies and bunny-rabbits painted on it.

It had been my old cot when I was a very small child and I had taken care of the pretty pictures. I used to kiss the fairies "good night" when I went to bed, but my bad little sister did not kiss them and take care of their pictures. Oh no!

My naughty little sister did dreadful things to those poor fairies. She scribbled on them with pencils and scratched them with tin-lids, and knocked them with poor old Rosy-primrose her doll, until there were hardly any pictures left at all. She said, "Nasty fairies. Silly old rabbits."

There! Wasn't she a bad child? You wouldn't do things like that, would you?

And my little sister jumped and jumped on her cot.
After she had been tucked up at night-time she would get
out from under the covers, and jump and jump. And when
she woke up in the morning she jumped and jumped again,
until one day, when she was jumping, the bottom fell

right out of the cot, and my naughty little sister, and the
mattress, and the covers, and poor Rosy-primrose all fell
out on to the floor!

Then our mother said, "That child must have a bed!"
Even though our father managed to mend the cot, our
mother said, "She must have a bed!"

My naughty little sister said, "A big bed for me?"

And our mother said, "I am afraid so, you bad child. You are too rough now for your poor old cot."

My little sister wasn't ashamed of being too rough for her cot. She was pleased because she was going to have the new bed, and she said, "A big girl's bed for me!"

My little sister told everybody that she was going to have a big girl's bed. She told her kind friend the window-cleaner man, and the coalman, and the milkman. She told the dustman too. She said, "You can have my old cot soon, dustman, because I am going to have a big girl's bed." And she was as pleased as pleased.

But our mother wasn't pleased at all. She was rather worried. You see, our mother was afraid that my naughty little sister would jump and jump on her new bed, and scratch it, and treat it badly. My naughty little sister had done such dreadful things to her old cot, that my mother was afraid she would spoil the new bed too.

Well now, my little sister told the lady who lived next door all about her new bed. The lady who lived next door to us was called Mrs Jones, but my little sister used to call her Mrs Cocoa Jones because she used to go in and have a cup of cocoa with her every morning.

Mrs Cocoa Jones was a very kind lady, and when she heard about the new bed she said, "I have a little yellow eiderdown and a yellow counterpane upstairs, and they are too small for any of my beds, so when your new bed comes, I will give them to you."

My little sister was excited, but when she told our mother what Mrs Cocoa had said, our mother shook her head.

"Oh dear," she said, "what will happen to the lovely eiderdown and counterpane when our bad little girl has them?"

Then a kind aunt who lived near us said, "I have a dear little green nightie-case put away in a drawer. It belonged to me when I was a little girl. When your new bed comes you can have it to put your nighties in like a big girl."

My little sister said, "Good. Good," because of all the nice things she was going to have for her bed. But our mother was more worried than ever. She said, "Oh dear! That pretty nightie-case. You'll spoil it, I know you will!"

But my little sister went on being pleased as pleased about it.

Then one day the new bed arrived. It was a lovely, shiny brown bed, new as new, with a lovely blue stripy mattress to go on it, new as new. And there was a new stripy pillow too. Just like a real big girl would have.

My little sister watched while my mother took the poor old cot to pieces, and stood it up against the wall. She watched when the new bed was put up, and the new mattress was laid on top of it. She watched the new pillow being put into a clean white case, and when our mother made the bed with clean new sheets and clean new blankets, she said, "Really big-girl! A big girl's bed – all for me."

44

Then Mrs Cocoa Jones came in, and she was carrying the pretty yellow eiderdown and the yellow counterpane. They were very shiny and satiny like buttercup flowers, and when our mother put them on top of the new bed, they looked beautiful.

Then our kind aunt came down the road, and *she* was carrying a little parcel, and in the little parcel was the pretty green nightie-case. My little sister ran down the road to meet her because she was so excited. She was more excited still when our aunt picked up her little nightdress and put it into the pretty green case and laid the green case on the yellow shiny eiderdown.

45

My little sister was so pleased that she was glad when bedtime came.

And, what do you think? She got carefully, carefully into bed with Rosy-primrose, and she laid herself down and stretched herself out – carefully, carefully like a good, nice girl.

And she didn't jump and jump, and she didn't scratch the shiny brown wood, or scribble with pencils or scrape with tin-lids. Not ever! Not even when she had had the new bed a long, long time.

My little sister took great care of her big girl's bed. She took great care of her shiny yellow eiderdown and counterpane and her pretty green nightie-case.

And whatever do you think she said to me?

She said, "You had the fairy pink cot before I did. But this is my very own big girl's bed, and I am going to take great care of my very own bed, like a big girl!"

7 · My naughty little sister and the baby

ONE DAY A lady called Mrs Rogers asked my mother if she would mind her little boy-baby for the afternoon.

My mother was very pleased to help Mrs Rogers. "I should be glad to mind the baby," she said.

I was very pleased to think we were going to have a little boy-baby in our house for a whole afternoon, but my little sister said, "I don't know babies, do I?"

Our mother said, "No, but I expect you will know this one quite well by the time Mrs Rogers comes for it. You can't help knowing babies," our mother said.

And my little sister said, "Well, I hope I am glad when I know it."

Well now, when Mrs Rogers came, my silly sister would not go out to look at the baby. She stood at the door and behaved in a very shy and peepy way and waited for our mother to call her.

"Come and look at the boy-baby," said Mother, and she took my sister to look at the baby in the pram.

He was a very dear baby. He was kicking and cooing and smiling and looking very happy.

"Isn't he nice?" my mother said.

My little sister didn't say, "Yes, he is nice" because she didn't know the baby very well then, she said, "He's very fat."

My mother told my little sister, "All babies are fat. *You* were fat too," she said.

My little sister was very surprised to hear that she had been fat like the boy-baby.

She stuck out her tummy and blew out her cheeks to look fat, and said, "Fat girl."

When the baby saw my little sister pretending to be fat he began to laugh, and when he laughed he showed a little white tooth. "Look, a toothy," said my little sister, and when she said "Look, a toothy", that little boy-baby laughed very loudly indeed, and he took off his white woolly cap and threw it right out of the pram!

My little sister picked up the white woolly cap for the baby.

"Put it back on his head," our mother said, and my little sister did put it back on his head, and do you know, the bad boy-baby pulled his cap straight off again and threw it out of the pram!

So – my little sister picked the cap up *again* – and put it on the boy-baby's head *again*, and that naughty boy pulled it off and threw it away and laughed and laughed,

48

and my little sister laughed as well because the boy-baby was so jolly and so fat.

Then my little sister talked to the baby. "You must keep your cap *on*," she said, and she pulled it on very carefully and tightly, and when he tried to pull it off again it only fell over one of his eyes.

Then my little sister put his cap straight, and *then* she

did a very clever thing to make him forget all about his cap. She popped her old doll, Rosy-primrose, round the side of the pram, and said, "Boh." And the boy-baby was so pleased he giggled and giggled.

So my little sister popped Rosy-primrose round the pram

again and again, and each time the funny baby giggled and my little sister giggled. Mother laughed and I laughed too to see my funny sister and the funny boy-baby.

Then my little sister said to the boy-baby, "What is your name?" and the boy-baby laughed again and said, "Ay-ay."

"Where do you live?" asked my little sister, and the boy-baby said "Ay-ay" again. Then the baby said, "Oigle, oigle, oigle," and my sister said, "That's a funny thing to say."

My mother said, "He doesn't talk properly yet. *You* didn't talk when you were a baby."

What a surprise for my naughty little sister. "Not talk!"

When tea-time came the baby sat in the old high-chair next to my naughty little sister, and my mother gave him some crusts with butter on them.

That bad baby dropped some of his crusts on the floor, and sucked some of them, and waved some of them about, and then he tried to push a crust into my little sister's ear. She was cross!

But our mother told her that the baby was too little to know any better, so my little sister forgave the baby and laughed at him.

When tea was over, the baby lay in his pram and played with his toes, and then he fell asleep. He was fast asleep when Mrs Rogers came to take him home.

When my naughty little sister went to bed that night,

do you know what she did? She pretended that she couldn't talk, she said, "Ay-ay, ay-ay," and played with her toes just like the boy-baby did.

Then she *did* speak; she said, "I know lots about babies now, don't I?"

8 · The fairy-doll

WHEN I WAS a little girl, I had a fairy-doll that was so beautiful that I never wanted to play with it.

It had real shiny wings and a shiny crown and a fairy-wand, and a sticking-out dress with golden stars on it, and it shut its eyes when you laid it down and opened them when you stood it up and said, "ma-ma," if you tipped it forwards.

It was so beautiful that I kept it in its box, wrapped up in white paper, in the drawer of my mother's wardrobe. I used to go and peep at it whenever I specially wanted to.

Well now, my naughty little sister had a doll too. Her doll was a very poor old thing, with no eyes left, and all its nose rubbed off. My naughty little sister called *her* doll "Rosy-primrose". My little sister used to take Rosy-primrose to bed with her, but sometimes, when my naughty little sister was cross, she would smack poor Rosy-primrose and throw her out of bed.

One day, when my naughty little sister threw Rosy-primrose out of bed, my mother said, "I think I'll take that poor old doll downstairs and put her in the cupboard until you can be kind to her."

But my naughty little sister said, "Won't be kind to her."
So my mother put Rosy-primrose away in the cupboard
for a rest.

Now, what do you think? The very next day, when my
mother was doing the ironing, she suddenly said, "Where
is that naughty little girl? Where is that naughty sister of
yours? I expect she's in mischief, because she is so quiet."
That's what my mother said.

So my mother stopped her ironing, and went out into
the garden to look for my little sister. But she wasn't in
the garden. My mother looked in the shed, and she wasn't

in the shed. She wasn't in the sitting-room, or in her bed-room, or in the spare room, but when my mother peeped into her own bedroom – there was my naughty little sister looking very cross at being caught.

The fairy-doll's box wasn't in the wardrobe drawer either. It was on the bed, and all the white paper was all over the floor, and there was my naughty little sister hold-ing my fairy-doll and making it say, "ma-ma, ma-ma, ma-ma, ma-ma."

My mother was very cross. She said, "That's not your doll. It belongs to your big sister," and my naughty little sister said, "I want it." My mother said, "Put it down on the bed," and my very naughty little sister said, "No."

Then my mother was angry, and went to take the doll away from my naughty little sister, but that bad child ran away with my lovely fairy-doll. And, well – you remember what she did to poor Rosy-primrose when she was cross, don't you? She did something even more dreadful to my fairy-doll. *She threw it out of the window*, that lovely beautiful doll with the golden wings and the shiny crown *and* the sticking-out dress with golden stars on.

My naughty little sister had to go straight to bed for that, because she really had been terrible.

My lovely fairy-doll had fallen down into the garden, right into a muddy puddle, and its face was broken. I cried and cried, and when my little sister saw the poor fairy-doll, she cried and cried too, because she wasn't

54

really such a bad child as all that – she just threw the doll out of the window when she was being mischievous.

My naughty little sister was so very sorry that we all forgave her, and my mother said that if she promised to be kind in future, she should have Rosy-primrose back very soon. So my little sister promised hard.

Do you know what my kind mother did? She sent the poor fairy-doll to the Doll's Hospital, and she sent Rosy-primrose there too, and when the two dolls came back, they looked very nice.

My little sister was a bit sorry to see Rosy-primrose, because Rosy-primrose had a new nice face and some curly hair that hadn't been there for a long, long time. My little sister never was quite happy with the tidy Rosy-primrose until it lost all its hair again, and its new eyes fell in. But she was always kind to it after that.

I was glad about my fairy-doll, though. Because it wasn't a fairy any more after the window-fall. It had a pretty new face, and a nice smile with teeth showing, and it *still* shut its eyes when you laid it down, and it *still* said, "ma-ma"; but the fairy-clothes had all been spoiled in the muddy puddle, so my mother made it a nice yellow dress and bonnet, and a white apron, and I called it "Anna-bella", and, now that its clothes were not so grand, I could play with it whenever I wanted to – so really that fairy-doll's window-fall wasn't so terribly dreadful after all.

9 · My naughty little sister and the sweep

ONE MORNING WHEN my naughty little sister and I went downstairs to breakfast we found everything looking very funny indeed.

The table was pushed right up against the wall, and the chairs were standing on the table and they were all covered over with a big sheet. The curtains were gone from the window, and the armchairs and the pictures and the clock and lots of other things. All gone!

My little sister was very interested to see all this, and when she looked out of the window, she saw that the arm-chairs and the pictures and all the other things were piled up in our back garden. My little sister *did* stare.

Clock and pictures and armchairs in the back garden, and things covered up with sheets; no curtains! Wasn't that a strange thing to find? My little sister said, "We have got a funny home today."

Then my mother told us that the chimney-sweep was coming to clean the chimney and that she had had to get the room ready for him. My naughty little sister was very excited because she had never seen a sweep, and she jumped and said "Sweep" and jumped and said "Sweep" again and again because she was so excited. Then she said, "Won't we have any breakfast?"

"Won't we have any breakfast?" said my hungry little sister, because the chairs were standing on the table. And Mother said, "As it is a lovely sunny morning you are going to have a picnic breakfast in the garden."

Then my little sister was very pleased indeed because she had never had a picnic breakfast before.

She said, "What shall we eat?" and my mother told her, "Well, as it is a special picnic breakfast, I have made you some egg sandwiches." Wasn't that nice? Sandwiches for breakfast! There was milk too, and bananas. My sister *did* like it!

We sat on the back doorstep and ate and ate and drank and drank because it was so nice to be eating our breakfast in the open air.

Then, just as my little sister finished her very last bite of banana, a big man with a black-dirty face came in the back gate and Mother said, "Here is the sweep at last."

Well, *you* know all about sweeps, but my little sister didn't, and she was so interested that my mother said she could watch the sweep so long as she didn't meddle in any way. My sister said she would be very good, so my mother found her one of my overalls, and tied a hanky round her head to keep her hair clean, and said, "Now you can go and watch the sweep."

My little sister watched the sweep man push the brush

up the chimney and she watched when he screwed a cane on to the brush and a cane on to that cane, and a cane on to that cane, all the time pushing the brush up and up the chimney, and she stayed as good as good. She was very quiet. She didn't say a thing.

She was so mousy-quiet that the black sweep man said, "You are quiet, missy; haven't you got a tongue?"

My sister was very surprised when the sweep asked if she had got a tongue, so she stuck her tongue out quickly to show that she had got one, and he said, "Fancy that now!"

Then my little sister laughed and the sweep laughed and she wasn't quiet any more. She talked and talked until he had finished his work.

Then my sister asked the sweep what he was going to do with all the soot he had collected and he said, "I shall leave it for your father to use in his garden. It's good for frightening off the tiddy little slugs."

So, when the sweep man went away he left a little pile of soot in the garden for our father. My sister was sorry when he went away, and she asked my mother lots of questions. She wanted to know so many things that Mother said, "If I answer you now I'll never get the place straight, so just you run off and play like a good girl, and I will tell you all about soot and chimney-sweeps later on."

So my sister went off, and Mother cleaned up the room and brought in the chairs and hung up curtains and did all the other tidying up things and all the time my sister was very quiet.

There had been lots of things my sister had wanted to know very badly. One thing she had wanted to know was if there was soot in *all* the chimneys. She wondered if there was any soot in her own bedroom chimney.

She went upstairs and looked up her chimney but she couldn't see because it was too dark up there.

It was very dark and my sister probably wouldn't have bothered any more about it, only she happened to remember that there was a long cane on the landing with a feather duster on the top, that Mother used for getting the cobwebs from the top of the stairs.

Yes, I thought you would guess. The cane was very bendy and it wasn't difficult for a little girl to push it up the chimney.

Have you ever done anything so very silly as this? If you have you will know how dirty soot is. It's much dirtier than mud even.

My silly sister pushed the feather duster up her bedroom chimney and a lot of soot fell down into the fireplace. It was such a lot of soot and it looked so dirty that my little sister got frightened and wished that she hadn't done such an awful thing.

She couldn't help thinking that Mother would be very cross when she saw it.

So she thought she had better hide it.

You will never guess where that silly child tried to hide the soot. *In her bed.*

Yes, in her own nice clean little comfortable bed.

I'm glad to think that you wouldn't be so silly.

My sister made such a mess carrying the soot across the room and touching things with her sooty fingers and treading on the floor with sooty feet that she didn't know what to do.

She saw how messy her bedroom was and she was very, very sorry; she was so sorry that she ran right downstairs to the garden where Mother was shaking the mats, and she flung her little sooty arms round Mother's skirt, and pushed her little sooty face into Mother's apron, and she said, "Oh, I have been a bad girl. I have been a bad girl. Scold me a lot. Scold me a lot." And then she cried and cried and cried and cried and *cried*.

And she was so sorry and so ashamed that Mother forgave her even though it made her a lot of extra work on a very busy day.

My little sister was so sorry that she fetched things and carried things and told Mother when the sheets were dry and helped to lay the table for dinner and behaved like the best child in England, so that our father said it was almost worth having her behave so badly when she could show afterwards what a good girl she really was.

Our father was a very funny man.

10 · My naughty little sister is very sorry

IN OUR ROAD lived a cross lady called Mrs Lock, and she didn't like children.

Mrs Lock didn't like children at all, and if she saw a boy or girl stopping by her front gate she would tap on her window to them and say, "Don't hang about here" in a very grumbling voice.

Wasn't that a cross thing to do? I will tell you why Mrs Lock was so cross. It was because she had a very beautiful garden outside her front door, and once some boys had been playing football in the roadway, and the ball had bounced into her garden and broken down a beautiful rose-tree.

So when Mrs Lock saw children by her gate she thought they were going to start playing with footballs and damage her garden, and she always sent them away.

Sometimes she came right out of the house and down to the gate and said, "Go and play in the park – the roadway is no place for games," and she would look so fierce and cross that the children would hurry away at once.

There was another reason, too, why Mrs Lock was so cross. You see, she had a beautiful smoky-looking cat, and one day a nasty child had thrown a stone at the cat and hurt his poor leg, so if Mrs Lock saw a boy or girl stroking her smoky-looking cat, she would say, "Don't you meddle with that cat, now!"

What a cross lady she was! But I suppose you couldn't really blame her. It isn't nice to have your rose-trees broken, and it's very, very bad to have your poor cat injured, isn't it?

Well now, one bright sunshiny morning my naughty little sister went out for a little walk down the road all by herself. It was only a very small walk, just as far as the lamp-post at the corner of the road and back again, but my little sister was pretending that it was a very long walk; she was pretending that she was a shopping-lady, stopping at all the hedges and gate-ways and saying that they were shops.

My little sister had a lovely game, all by herself, being a shopping-lady. It was a very nice day, and she had a little cane shopping-basket just like our mother's and a little old purse full of beads for pennies.

First my little sister stopped at a hedge and said, "I'll have a nice cabbage today, please." Then she picked a leaf and pretended that it was a cabbage, and put it carefully into her basket. She took two beads out of her purse and left them under the hedge to pay for it.

She went on until she came to a wall; there were two little round stones by the wall, so she pretended that they were eggs and bought them too.

Then she found a piece of red flower-pot which made nice meat for her pretend-dinner. She had a lovely game.

Just as she arrived at Mrs Lock's gate, the big smoky-looking cat jumped up on to it and began to purr and purr, and as he purred his big feathery tail went all curly and twisty and he looked very beautiful. My sister stopped to look at him.

When the big smoky-looking cat saw my sister looking at him, he opened his mouth and showed her all his sharp little teeth; then he stretched out his curly pink tongue and began to lick one of his legs. He licked and licked.

My little sister was very pleased to see such a nice cat and she stood tippy-toe and touched him. When she did this he stopped licking and began to purr again. He was nice and warm and furry, so she stroked him, very gently towards his tail because Mother had told us that pussies didn't like being stroked the other way. "Dear pussy. Nice animal," she said to him.

Now, as my sister was such a little girl Mrs Lock didn't see her standing by the gate, so she didn't say "go away" to her, and my sister had a long talk with the smoky-looking cat.

She told him that she was a shopping-lady. "I have bought lots of things," she said. "I can't think of anything else."

When she said this, the cat got up suddenly and jumped right off the gate back into Mrs Lock's garden, and as he jumped the gate opened wide. "Miaow," he said. "Miaow" – like that.

My bad little sister looked through the gate and she saw

the smoky cat going up the path. She saw all the pretty tulip flowers and the wallflowers growing on each side, and do you know what she said?

She said, "That was very kind of you, Pussy. Now I can buy a nice cup to drink my milk out of."

And she walked into Mrs Lock's garden. Mrs Lock's tulip flowers were all different colours: red, yellow, pink and white. You know that tulip flowers look rather like cups, don't you?

Yes. You know.

"I'll have a yellow cup, please," my bad sister said. "Here's the money, Pussy."

And she picked a yellow tulip head and put it in her basket.

The smoky-looking cat walked round and round her legs, and his long tickly tail waved and waved and he said, "Purr" to my little sister who was pretending to be a shopping-lady.

And Mrs Lock saw her from her front window.

Mrs Lock *was* cross. She tapped hard on her window glass and my naughty little sister saw her. Then she remembered that she wasn't really a shopping-lady, she remembered that she was a little girl. She remembered that it was naughty to pick flowers that didn't belong to you.

Of course you know what she did? Yes. She ran away, through the gate and down the road to our house, while

68

Mrs Lock tapped and tapped and the smoky cat stood still in surprise. My little sister ran straight indoors and straight

upstairs and hid herself under the bed.

Mrs Lock came down the road after her, and when she saw my little sister run into the house, she came and knocked at our door, and told our mother all about my little sister's bad behaviour.

My mother was very sorry to hear that my sister had picked one of Mrs Lock's tulips, and when Mrs Lock had gone, our mother went upstairs and peeped under the bed.

You see, she knew *just* where her naughty little girl would be.

"Come out," Mother said in a kind voice, because she

knew my little sister was ashamed of herself, and my little sister came out very slowly, and stood by the side of the bed and looked very sad; but Mother was so nice that my sister told her all about the pretending game and the pussy cat, and Mother explained to her that you have to think even when you're pretending hard, and not do naughty things by mistake.

Then she told my sister all about why Mrs Lock was cross. About her rose-tree and the nasty thing that had happened to the smoky-looking cat. And my sister was very, very sorry.

When Mother went downstairs again my sister had a good idea. She went to her toy-box and she found the beautiful card that our granny had sent her for her birthday. It had a pretty picture of a pussy cat and a bunch of

roses on it. It was the nicest card my sister had ever had, but she thought she would give it to Mrs Lock to show that she was sorry.

She didn't say a word to anyone. She went out very quietly down the road to Mrs Lock's gate.

When she got there, my little sister went inside the gate and up the path. The smoky-looking cat came round the side of the house to meet her, but she didn't stop to stroke him. No. She went up to Mrs Lock's front door, and rattled the letter box; then she pushed the postcard inside. She put her mouth close to the letter box and shouted, "I am sorry I took your flower, Mrs Lock. I am very-very sorry. I have brought you my best postcard for a present."

And then she ran away again. Only this time Mrs Lock didn't tap the glass.

The very next time my little sister went by Mrs Lock's gate there was Mrs Lock herself, pulling weeds out of her pathway, and there was the smoky-looking cat sitting on a gatepost. When the cat saw my little sister he jumped down from the gatepost and said "purr" to her and rubbed round and round her legs. Then Mrs Lock stood up very straight and looked over the gate at my little sister.

Mrs Lock said, "Thank you for the card."

All the time the smoky-coloured cat was purring and rubbing, rubbing and purring round and round my sister's legs and Mrs Lock said, "My cat likes you. His name is Tibbles. Stroke him."

And my sister did stroke him, and after that she stroked him every time she went past Mrs Lock's gate and found him sitting there in the sunshine. And although Mrs Lock often saw her stroking him she never said "Don't you meddle with my cat" to her.

And when Christmas time came Mrs Lock sent my sister a card with robins and holly and shiny glittery stuff on it that was even more lovely than the pussy-cat card.

I I · Bad Harry and the milkman

MY NAUGHTY LITTLE sister had a friend called Harry. Harry was a naughty boy, so he and my sister were very good friends.

Harry and my sister were very noisy when they played together. If they saw anything funny they would laugh and laugh and roll about on the ground, and they always laughed at the same time at the same thing.

And when my sister was cross, Harry was cross, and when she was stubborn, he was stubborn too, and when she said, "*I* want that!" about something, Harry always said, "You can't have it, because *I* want it."

My sister would shout, "Give it to me at once!" and Harry would shout, "No".

Then my sister would jump up and down and say, "Bad Harry" over and over again. "Bad, bad, Harry!"

Then she would pull his hair, and he would pull her hair and they would hit each other in a very unkind way, until our mother came out and grumbled at them. Then they would stop fighting.

But they went on being friends just the same.

73

But when Harry came to our house or she went to Harry's house, she had to say "Bad Harry" so many times that we called him Bad Harry in the end, and he really was, bad as bad. Oh dear.

They were cross good friends, weren't they?

Well now, when my sister and Harry were very small, they didn't come visiting each other on their own. Our mother took my sister to Harry's house, and Harry's mother brought him round to us, and as our mothers were busy women they couldn't always be walking round to each other's houses, so there were some days when Harry and my sister couldn't see each other and they didn't like that at all.

One day, when it was cold and snowy, Harry's poor mother wasn't a very well lady, and she couldn't go out, so Harry had to stop at home and not see my sister, and he didn't like that.

Harry stood and looked out of the window, and saw the snow coming down, and everything looking very white and pretty, and he thought of all the lovely games he could have in the snow with my sister.

He thought of making snowballs and throwing them at her, as he'd seen the big boys making snowballs and throwing them at their friends, and he thought of them making a funny old snowman with a pipe like a picture in one of his books. He thought of all sorts of nice games in the snow.

Then he got very cross and miserable in case the snow

should melt before he could play with my sister again.

Then Harry had a bad idea (not a good idea – a *bad* one). He thought he would put on his coat and hat and go

and visit my sister all on his own.

What a very bad Harry.

The next-door lady who had come in to make Harry's breakfast had gone home for a little while, and his mother was fast asleep in bed upstairs, so there was no one to ask.

Bad Harry went and fetched his coat and put it on. He wasn't good about buttons then, so he left it undone.

He found his woolly cap and he put that on. He forgot

75

his gloves, and his leggings and his shoes. He was in such a hurry.

He opened the front door, and off he went in his bunny-slippers down the path and out into the snow. He *was* excited; he hurried to get to our house to play with my sister.

The snow fell and fell. It was swirly and curly and cold and it blew into Harry's face, and it crunched under his bunny-slippers, and he thought it was very exciting.

Now all the people who lived in Harry's road had very kindly swept the snow from the pavements in front of their houses so it was quite easy for Harry to get along, but when he turned the first corner, he came to a road where the people hadn't been so kind and thoughtful about clearing the pavements, and soon his little bunny-slippers were quite covered up when he walked.

And his feet got wet and cold.

The wind was blowing down that street too, and it threw the snow into Harry's face in a very unkind way, and Harry suddenly found that his fingers were cold too.

His feet were cold and his fingers were cold, and he hadn't done his coat up so he was all cold. Cold as cold.

And because he was only a little boy then, Harry did a silly little-boy thing. He stood quite still. He opened his mouth and he started to cry and cry.

Now, we had a very nice milkman who came to our house. He was a great friend of my little sister's. This

milkman had an old white horse and a jingly cart and when he came down the road he would call out "MILK-O! M-I-L-K-O!"

Like that, and when he came to the door he would sing, "Milk for the babies, cream for the ladies! M-I-L-K-O!" He was a nice milkman.

He was *just* the person to come along with his white horse and jingly cart and find poor Bad Harry crying because he was cold.

Down the road he came, jingle jingle rather slowly because of the snow on the road, and his old white horse walking carefully, carefully. And he saw Harry.

He saw cold Harry crying so he said, "Who-a there" to his old white horse, and the milk-cart stopped and he got down and said, "Why, you're the little chap who plays with young Saucy down the next street."

When the milkman said "young Saucy down the next street" he meant my sister, because he always called her that (although it wasn't her name, of course).

When the nice milkman saw how cold poor Harry was, and how miserable he was, he put him into his milk-cart and wrapped him up in a rug that was on the seat, and because he didn't know where Harry lived, he took him round to our house, which wasn't very far away – only round the next corner after all!

Now my sister was standing by *our* kitchen window being as cross as cross, and wanting to play in the snow

78

with Harry, when she saw the milkman stopping at the gate.

She was very surprised when she saw him lift a bundle in a rug out of his cart and carry it up our path, so she ran to the door with Mother to see what it was all about.

When they opened the door they heard Harry bellowing and crying because he was so cold, and Mother thanked the milkman for bringing him and took him in quickly to warm by our fire.

Poor Harry! Mother rubbed and rubbed him and gave him hot milk and made him sit with his feet in a bowl of hot water, until he stopped crying and told her that he had come round all on his own.

My sister opened her eyes wide when she heard this! On his own!

Mother told Harry that he had been *very naughty*. She said his mother might be very, very worried, and she sent me round at once to tell Harry's next-door lady where he was.

My sister stared hard at Harry when our mother told him he had been naughty and that his mother would be worried. When our mother scolded Harry he began to cry again, and this time my naughty little sister cried as well.

And they made so much noise that Mother forgave Harry and fetched him a biscuit, and he stopped crying.

My sister stopped crying too, and Mother gave her a biscuit, and they sat quiet as quiet until I came back with

Harry's shoes and some dry socks and leggings for him to put on, so that I could take him home again.

I told him that his next-door lady had said that his mother was still asleep and if we hurried we could get back before the poor not-well lady woke up.

So Harry hurried back with me and he was home again before his mother could wake up and worry.

Next day it was even more cold, and when the milkman came my sister saw that he had put some funny little red-woollen-bag things on his horse's ears.

She said, "Why has your horse got those funny bag things, milkman?"

And the nice milkman laughed and said, "In case we have to pick up that bad friend of yours again. He yelled so much he made my horse's ears twitch. He might give her ear-ache next time."

And my sister looked very good, and she said in a very good quiet voice, "I am afraid Harry is a Bad Boy."

12 · Bad Harry's haircut

WHEN HARRY WAS a bit bigger, as he only lived a little way away from us, and as there were no nasty roads to cross between our houses, he used to come all on his own to play with my little sister, and she used to go all on her own to play with him. And they were Very Good Friends.

And they were both very naughty children. Oh dear!

But if you could have seen this Bad Harry you wouldn't have said that he was a naughty child. He looked so very good. Yes, he looked very good indeed.

My little sister never looked very good, even when she was behaving herself, but Bad Harry looked good all the time.

My naughty little sister's friend Harry had big, big blue eyes and pretty golden curls like a baby angel, but oh dear, he was quite naughty all the same.

Now one day, when my little sister went round to play with Harry, she found him looking very smart indeed. He was wearing real big boy's trousers. Real ones, with real big boy's buttons and real big boy's braces! Red braces like a very big boy! Wasn't he smart?

"Look," said Bad Harry. "Look at my big boy's trousers."

"Smart," said my naughty little sister, "smart boy."

"I'm going to have a real boy's haircut too," said Bad Harry. "Today. Not Mummy with scissors any more; but a real boy's haircut in a real barber's shop!"

My word, he was a proud boy!

My little sister was *so* surprised, and Bad Harry was *so* pleased to see how surprised she was.

"I'll be a big boy then," he said.

Then Harry's mother, who was a kind lady and liked my little sister very much, said that if she was a good girl she could come to the barber's and see Harry have his haircut.

My little sister was so excited that she ran straight back home at once to tell our mother all about Harry's big boy's trousers and Harry's real boy's haircut.

"Can I go too, can I go too?" she asked our mother.

Our mother said, "Yes, you may go, only hold very tight to Harry's mother's hand when you cross the High Street," and my little sister promised that she would hold very tight indeed.

So off they went to the barber's to get Harry a Real Boy's Haircut.

My little sister had never been in a barber's shop before and she stared and stared. Bad Harry had never been in a barber's shop before either, but he didn't stare; he pretended that he knew all about it. He picked up one of the barber's books and pretended to look at the pictures in it, but he peeped all the time at the barber's shop.

There were three haircut-men in the barber's shop, and they all had white coats and they all had black combs sticking out of their pockets.

There were three white wash-basins with shiny taps and looking-glasses, and three very funny chairs. In the three funny chairs were three men all having something done to them by the three haircut-men.

One man was having his hair cut with scissors, and one man was having his neck clipped with clippers, and one man had a soapy white face and *he* was being shaved!

And there were bottles and bottles, and brushes and brushes, and towels and towels, and pretty pictures with writing on them, and all sorts of things to see! My little sister looked and Bad Harry peeped until it was Harry's turn to have his hair cut.

When it was Harry's turn one of the haircut-men fetched a special high-chair for Harry to sit in, because the grown-up chairs were all too big.

Harry sat in the special chair and then the haircut-man got a big blue sheet and wrapped it round Harry and tucked it in at the neck.

"You don't want any tickly old hairs going down there," the haircut-man said.

Then the haircut-man took his sharp shiny scissors and began to cut and cut. And down fell a golden curl and "Gone!" said my little sister, and down fell another golden curl and "Gone!" said my little sister again, and she said "Gone!" "Gone!" "Gone!" all the time until Harry's curls had quite gone away.

Then she said, "All gone now!"

When the haircut-man had finished cutting, he took a bottle with a squeezer-thing and he squirted some nice smelly stuff all over Harry's head and made Harry laugh, and my little sister laughed as well.

Then the haircut-man took the big black comb, and he made a Big Boy's Parting on Harry's head, and he combed Harry's hair back into a real boy's haircut, and then Bad Harry climbed down from the high-chair so that my little sister could really look at him.

And then my little sister *did* stare. Bad Harry's mother stared too. . . .

For there was that bad boy Harry, with his real boy's trousers and his real boy's braces, with a real boy's haircut, smiling and smiling, and looking very pleased.

"No curls now," said Bad Harry. "Not any more."

85

"No curls," said my naughty little sister.

"No," Bad Harry's mother said, "and oh dear! you don't even *look* good any more."

Then my little sister laughed and laughed. "Bad Harry!" she said. "Bad Harry. All bad now – like me!"

$I3$ · My naughty little sister at the party

YOU WOULDN'T THINK there could be another child as naughty as my naughty little sister, would you? But there was. There was a thoroughly bad boy who was my naughty little sister's best boy-friend: Bad Harry.

This Bad Harry and my naughty little sister used to play together quite a lot in Harry's garden, or in our garden, and got up to dreadful mischief between them, picking all the baby gooseberries, and the green blakccurrants, and throwing sand on the flower-beds, and digging up the runner-bean seeds, and all the naughty sorts of things you never, never do in the garden.

Now, one day this Bad Harry's birthday was near, and Bad Harry's mother said he could have a birthday-party and invite lots of children to tea. So Bad Harry came round to our house with a pretty card in an envelope for my naughty little sister, and this card was an invitation asking my naughty little sister to come to the birthday-party.

Bad Harry told my naughty little sister that there would

be a lovely tea with jellies and sandwiches and birthday-cake, and my naughty little sister said, "Jolly good."

And every time she thought about the party she said, "Nice tea and birthday-cake." Wasn't she greedy? And when the party-day came she didn't make any fuss when my mother dressed her in her new green party-dress, and her green party-shoes and her green hair-ribbon, and she didn't fidget and she didn't wriggle her head about when she was having her hair combed, she kept as still as still, because she was so pleased to think about the party, and when my mother said, "Now, what must you say at the party?" my naughty little sister said, "I must say, 'nice tea'. "

But my mother said, "No, no, that *would* be a greedy thing to say. You must say 'please' and 'thank you' like a good polite child, at tea-time, and say, 'thank you very much for having me,' when the party is over."

And my naughty little sister said, "All right, Mother, I promise."

So my mother took my naughty little sister to the party, and what do you think the silly little girl did as soon as she got there? She went up to Bad Harry's mother and she said very quickly, "Please-and-thank-you, and-thank-you-very-much-for-having-me," all at once – just like that, before she forgot to be polite, and then she said, "Now, may I have a lovely tea?"

Wasn't that rude and greedy? Bad Harry's mother said, "I'm afraid you will have to wait until all the other children are here, but Harry shall show you the tea-table if you like."

Bad Harry looked very smart in a blue party-suit, with white socks and shoes and a real boy's haircut, and he said, "Come on, I'll show you."

So they went into the tea-room and there was the birthday-tea spread out on the table. Bad Harry's mother had made red jellies and yellow jellies, and blancmanges

and biscuits and sandwiches and cakes-with-cherries-on, and a big birthday-cake with white icing on it and candles, and "Happy Birthday, Harry", written on it.

My naughty little sister's eyes grew bigger and bigger, and Bad Harry said, "There's something else in the larder. It's going to be a surprise treat, but you shall see it because you are my best girl-friend."

So bad Harry took my naughty little sister out into the kitchen and they took chairs and climbed up to the larder shelf – which is a dangerous thing to do, and it would have been their own faults if they had fallen down – and Bad Harry showed my naughty little sister a lovely spongy trifle, covered with creamy stuff and with silver balls and jelly-sweets on the top. And my naughty little sister stared more than ever because she liked spongy trifle better than jellies or blancmanges or biscuits or sandwiches or cakes-with-cherries-on, or even birthday-cake, so she said, "For me."

Bad Harry said, "For me too," because he liked spongy trifle best as well.

Then Bad Harry's mother called to them and said, "Come along, the other children are arriving."

So they went to say, "How do you do!" to the other children, and then Bad Harry's mother said, "I think we will have a few games now before tea – just until everyone has arrived."

All the other children stood in a ring and Bad Harry's mother said, "Ring O'Roses first, I think." And all the nice party children said, "Oh, we'd like that."

But my naughty little sister said, "No Ring O'Roses – nasty Ring O'Roses" – just like that, because she didn't like Ring O'Roses very much, and Bad Harry said, "Silly game."

So Bad Harry and my naughty little sister stood and

watched the others. The other children sang beautifully too, they sang,

"Ring O'Ring O'Roses,
A pocket full of posies —
A-tishoo, a-tishoo, we all fall down."

And they all fell down and laughed, but Harry and my naughty little sister didn't laugh. They got tired of watching and they went for a little walk. Do you know where they went to?

Yes. To the larder. To take another look at the spongy trifle. They climbed up on to the chairs to look at it really properly. It was very pretty.

"Ring O'Ring O'Roses" sang the good party children.

"Nice jelly-sweets," said my naughty little sister. "Nice silver balls," and she looked at that terribly Bad Harry and he looked at her.

"Take one," said that naughty boy, and my naughty little sister did take one, she took a red jelly-sweet from the top of the trifle; and then Bad Harry took a green jelly-sweet; and then my naughty little sister took a yellow jelly-sweet and a silver ball, and then Bad Harry took three jelly-sweets, red, green and yellow, and six silver balls, one, two, three, four, five, six, and put them all in his mouth at once.

Now some of the creamy stuff had come off upon Bad

Harry's fingers and he liked it very much, so he put his
finger into the creamy stuff on the trifle, and took some of
it off and ate it, and my naughty little sister ate some too.
I'm sorry to have to tell you this, because I feel so ashamed
of them, and expect you feel ashamed of them too.

I hope you aren't too shocked to hear any more?
Because, do you know, those two bad children forgot all
about the party and the nice children all singing "Ring

O'Roses". They took a spoon each and scraped off the creamy stuff and ate it, and then they began to eat the nice spongy inside.

Bad Harry said, "Now we've made the trifle look so untidy, no one else will want any, so we may as well eat it all up." So they dug away into the spongy inside of the trifle and found lots of nice fruity bits inside. It was a very big trifle, but those greedy children ate and ate.

Then, just as they had nearly finished the whole big trifle, the "Ring O'Roses"-ing stopped, and Bad Harry's mother called, "Where are you two? We are ready for tea."

Then my naughty little sister was very frightened. Because she knew she had been very naughty, and she looked at Bad Harry and *he* knew *he* had been very naughty, and they both felt terrible. Bad Harry had a creamy mess of trifle all over his face, and even in his real boy's haircut, and my naughty little sister had made her new green party-dress all trifly – you know how it happens if you eat too quickly and greedily.

"It's tea-time," said Bad Harry, and he looked at my naughty little sister, and my naughty little sister thought of the jellies and the cakes and the sandwiches, and all the other things, and she felt very full of trifle, and she said, "Don't want any."

And do you know what she did? Just as Bad Harry's mother came into the kitchen, my naughty little sister slipped out of the door, and ran and ran all the way home.

It was a good thing our home was only down the street and no roads to cross, or I don't know what would have happened to her.

Bad Harry's mother was so cross when she saw the trifle, that she sent Bad Harry straight to bed, and he had to stay there and hear all the nice children enjoying themselves. I don't know what happened to him in the night, but I know that my naughty little sister wasn't at all a well girl, from having eaten so much trifle – and I also know that she doesn't like spongy trifle any more.

I4 · My naughty little sister shows off

DO YOU LIKE climbing? My naughty little sister used to like climbing very much indeed. She climbed up fences and on chairs and down ditches and round railings, and my mother used to say, "One day that child will fall and hurt herself."

But our father said, "She will be all right if she is careful."

And my little sister *was* careful. She didn't want to hurt herself. She climbed on *easy things*, and when she knew she had gone far enough, she always came down again, slowly, slowly, carefully, carefully – one foot down – the other foot down – like that.

My little sister was so careful about climbing that our father nailed a piece of wood on to our front gate, so that she would have something to stand on when she wanted to look over it. There was a tree by the gate, and Father put an iron handle on the tree to help her to hold on tight. Wasn't he a kind daddy?

95

Well now, one day my naughty little sister went down to the front gate because she thought it would be nice to see all the people going by.

She climbed up carefully, carefully, like a good girl, and she held on to the iron handle, and she watched all the people going down the street.

First the postman came along. He said, "Hello, Monkey," and that made her laugh. She said, "Hello, postman, have you any letters for this house?" and the postman said, "Not today, I'm afraid, Monkey."

My little sister laughed again because the postman

called her "Monkey", but she remembered to hold on tight.

Then Mr Cocoa Jones went by on his bicycle. Mr Cocoa said, "Don't fall," and he ling-a-linged his bicycle bell at her. "Be very careful," said Mr Cocoa Jones, and "ling-a-ling," said Mr Cocoa Jones' bell.

My naughty little sister said, "I won't fall. I won't fall, Mr Cocoa. I'm sensible," and Mr Cocoa ling-a-linged his bell again and called "Good-bye".

My naughty little sister waved to Mr Cocoa. She waved very carefully. She didn't lean forward to see him go round the corner or anything silly like that. No, she was most careful.

She was careful when the nice baker came with the bread. She climbed down, carefully, carefully and let him in.

She was careful when cars went by. She held tight and stood very still. She saw a steam-roller and a rag-a'-bone man, and she held very tight indeed.

Then my naughty little sister saw her friend, Bad Harry, coming down the road, and she forgot to be sensible. She began to show off.

My little sister shouted, "Harry, Harry, look at me. I'm on the gate, Harry."

Bad Harry did look at her, because she called in such a loud voice, "Look at me!" like that.

Then my silly little sister stood on one leg only – just

because she wanted Bad Harry to think that she was a clever girl.

That made Bad Harry laugh, so my little sister showed off again. She stood on the other leg only, and then – she let go of the tree and waved her arms.

And then – she fell right off the gate. Bump! She fell down and bumped her head.

Oh dear! Her head *did* hurt, and my poor little sister

cried and cried. Bad Harry cried too, and my mother came hurrying out of the house to see what had happened.

Our dear mother said, "Don't cry, don't cry, baby," in a kind, kind voice. "Don't cry, baby dear," she said, and she picked my little sister up and took her indoors and Bad Harry followed them. They were still crying and crying.

They cried so much that my mother gave them each a sugar lump to suck. Then they stopped crying because they found that they couldn't cry and suck at the same time.

Then our mother looked at my sister's poor head. "What a nasty bruise," our mother said. "I think I had better put something on it for you, and you must be a good brave girl while I do it."

My little sister was a good brave girl, too. She held Bad Harry's hand very tight, and she shut her eyes while Mother put some stingy stuff out of a bottle on to her poor head. Our mother did it very quickly, and my brave sister didn't fidget and she didn't cry. Wasn't she good?

When our mother had finished she gave my little sister and her friend, Bad Harry, an apple each and they went into the garden to play.

They had a lovely time playing in the garden. First they picked dandelions and put them in the water-tub for boats. Then they played hide-and-seek among the cabbages. Then they made a little house underneath the apple-tree. Then they found some blue chalk and drew funny old men on the tool-shed door.

And my little sister forgot all about her poor head.

When our father came home and saw my naughty little sister playing in the garden he said, "Hello, old lady, have you been in the wars?" and my little sister was surprised because she had forgotten all about falling off the gate. Father said, "You have got a nasty lump on top!"

So my little sister thought she would go indoors and look at her nasty lump. She climbed up on to a chair to look at herself in the mirror on the kitchen wall, and she saw that there was a big bump on her forehead. It was all yellowy-greeny.

Our mother said, "Climbing again! I should think you would have had enough climbing for one day!"

My little sister looked at her big bump in the mirror, and then she climbed down from the chair, carefully, carefully.

She climbed down very carefully indeed, and do you know what she said? She said, "I like climbing very much, but I don't like falling down. And I *certainly* don't like nasty bumps on my head. So I don't think I will be a showing off girl any more."

15 · The very old birthday party

LONG AGO, WHEN my sister was a naughty little girl, we had a very old, old great-Auntie who lived in a big house with lots of other very old ladies and gentlemen.

Our mother used to go and visit this old Auntie sometimes and she used to tell us all about her. Then, one day our mother said, "How would you like to come with me to visit Dear Old Auntie?"

Our mother said, "She is going to have a birthday party next week, and I think it would be very nice if you little girls could come to it. You see it is a very special party because old Auntie will be one hundred years old."

One hundred years! That is very, very old. You ask some big person to tell you how old that means.

Well, *I* knew how old a hundred years was, so I said, "Good gracious, what an old lady!"

My sister didn't know how old it was then because she was so little, but she said, "good gracious" too, because I had.

"She is a very sweet little old lady," our mother told us.

"Everyone likes her. The lady who looks after all the old ladies and gentlemen says that Dear Old Auntie is the pride of the Home."

Wasn't that a nice thing for our old Auntie to be? The pride of the Home. We thought it was anyway, and we were very pleased to think that we were going to visit such a dear old lady on her one hundredth birthday.

Well now, when the birthday came, we were both very excited. We wore our best Sunday dresses and looked very smart girls.

Our mother had told us that we might take some money from our money-boxes to buy a present for our Dear Old

Auntie in the Woolworth's shop. Our mother let us choose our own presents too. I bought our Dear Old Auntie a nice little white handkerchief with blue flowers on the corner.

It took me a long time to think what to buy.

But my little sister didn't think at all. She knew just

what she wanted. She said, "I am going to buy one of those glassy-looking things with the little houses inside that make it snow when you shake them."

My little sister had been to the Woolworth's shop with Mrs Cocoa, so she knew all about these glassy things.

Do you know about them? They are very pretty.

I thought it was a silly thing to give to such a very old lady, but my naughty little sister said, "It isn't silly. I would like one of those glassy things for *my* birthday!"

And she said she wouldn't buy anything else, so our mother took her along to the toy-counter and let her pay for one of the glassy things with her own money.

So, when we went to visit the Birthday Old Lady we had some nice presents for her. I had the handkerchief and my sister had the glassy thing with the snow inside it, and Mother had a box of sweeties from my father, and a nice woollen shawl that Mrs Cocoa Jones had kindly knitted from some wool that Mother had bought.

Wasn't she a lucky old lady?

My sister and I had never been to an old people's Home before, so we were very quiet and staring when we got there.

There were so many old people. Dear old ladies and dear old gentlemen all with white hair and smiling faces, and they all talked to us and waved to us and shook hands with us in a very friendly way.

And we smiled too. My sister smiled and smiled.

The lady who looked after the old people was called Miss Simmons and she was very kind.

"We are all very glad to see such young people," she said to my sister. "Do you know I don't think we've ever had anyone quite as young as you before?"

My sister was very pleased to think that she was the first very young visitor, and she did something that she sometimes did to Mr and Mrs Cocoa Jones. *She blew kisses.* She was being nice.

Our dear old great-Auntie was sitting by the fire in a big chair, and when Miss Simmons took us over to meet her, she was very pleased to see us.

What a very little old wrinkly pretty lady our old Auntie was! She had a tiny soft little voice and twinkly little eyes and she took a great fancy to my naughty sister at once. She asked her to sit next to her.

104

Wasn't that a nice thing for my sister to be asked to do?

The old Auntie was very pleased with her presents. She put the shawl on straight away, and she put my handkerchief into her sleeve straight away too. But when she saw what my sister had brought she clapped her hands together in a funny old-lady way and she said: "Well-well-well. What a lovely treat! I haven't seen one of these since I was a little girl. I saw one in another little girl's house and I always wanted one. Now I've got one at last!"

And the dear old lady shook up the glassy thing and made the snow fall on to the little house, and then she shook it again and made the snow fall again.

She did it so many times that we knew how very pleased she was.

"Just fancy," she said, "I wanted one when I was a little girl like you, and I've got one today on my hundredth birthday."

Miss Simmons said, "I see you have a box of sweeties too. But I don't think you had better eat them yet. We have a birthday cake with one hundred candles for you to cut and a very nice birthday tea. It would be a pity to eat sweeties and spoil your appetite."

Now my sister had heard Mother say that sort of thing to her but she was surprised to think that people had to say such things to old ladies, and she stared rather hard at her dear old Auntie.

And what do you think? When kind Miss Simmons

went off to see about the birthday tea, old Auntie opened
her box of sweeties, and gave one to me and one to my
sister and then she ate one herself!

And she laughed and my sister laughed.

When Miss Simmons came back and saw what old
Auntie had done she shook her finger at her. "You are a
very naughty old lady," Miss Simmons said.

Then Miss Simmons looked at the hundred-years-old lady, and my bad little sister, both laughing together and she said, "Goodness me, you can see you are relations. You both look alike!"

And do you know, when I looked, and Mother looked, at the naughty old lady and my naughty little sister, we saw that they did!

16 · My naughty little sister and the good polite child

ONE DAY MY mother said to my naughty little sister, "I have a little girl coming to tea this afternoon. I hope you will be good and kind to her, because I am going to mind her while her mother goes out."

My little sister was very interested about this little girl, and my mother said, "Her name is Winnie and she is a good polite child, I hear."

So my little sister got all her toys out and put them in the garden to show Winnie when she came, and my mother made some cherry cakes and jam-tarts, and some ginger biscuits for tea.

Wasn't my mother a kind woman, making those nice things for tea? Do you know, because Winnie was coming, my mother said, "We will have tea in the garden, with the best bluebird tablecloth."

My little sister liked this, because the bluebird table-cloth was very special. It had bluebirds on it, and trees on it, and little funny men walking on bridges on it, and little boats with men fishing on it, and they were all blue as blue. My little sister said, "I shall like that."

When it was time for Winnie to come, my mother changed my little sister's dress, and put her on a pair of nice blue socks. My little sister was very proud of those

blue socks, and when she heard the knock at the front door she ran to show them to the good polite Winnie.

But what do you think? Winnie had blue socks too! And a blue silky dress, and blue shiny shoes, and when she came in, her mother put her a frilly white silky apron on to keep her dress clean. My little sister was so pleased to see how pretty Winnie looked that she forgot to say, "How do you do?" She said, "Blue socks too!" instead.

But do you know, that Winnie didn't say anything! She just stood and stood, and she didn't look at our mother, or my little sister, she just peeped. She made her eyes all peepy and small, because she didn't like to look at anyone, and when her mother went away, she didn't scream for her, or shout, "Good-bye," to her, or make any noise and fuss of any kind. She just went on being thoroughly peepy, and she went quietly, quietly into the garden with my little sister without saying anything at all.

My little sister showed Winnie all her toys. She showed her Rosy-primrose first. Rosy-primrose wasn't very beautiful that day, because it was a time when she had lost her hair and her eyes, and Winnie just peeped at Rosy-primrose and didn't say anything.

So my little sister showed her the bricks, and the story-books and the teddies and the patty tins, and the tea-set and the jig-saws, and all the other toys, and the good polite child didn't say anything at all.

So my funny little sister said, "Can you talk?" and then Winnie said, "Yes," to show she could speak, so my little sister said, "Would you like to make mud-pies?"

That good Winnie said, "Oh, no, I might get dirty." She didn't say "Yes" because she didn't want to get her beautiful dress and her beautiful apron dirty, so my little sister said, "Well, shall we go down the garden and eat gooseberries?" even though she knew that was naughty.

But good Winnie said, "No, I might get tummy-ache."

So my little sister said, "Shall we have a race round the lawn?" and Winnie said, "Oh, no, it's *so* hot," in a quiet good voice.

And she didn't want to climb up the apple-trees in case she tore her frock, and she didn't want to sit on the grass in case there were ants, and she didn't want to shout over the front gate to the schoolchildren because it was rude, and all the time she just looked peepy, peepy at my little sister.

So then my little sister said, "What would you like to do?" And the polite good Winnie said she would like to take a story-book indoors to read. So she took one of the story-books indoors and read it on her own.

My naughty little sister didn't want to read story-books indoors, so she went and made a dirt-pie, and ate some gooseberries, and raced round the lawn, and climbed the apple-trees, and sat on the grass, and then she shouted over the gate at the schoolchildren, just to show how bad she could be.

When tea-time came, with all the nice cherry cakes and jam-tarts and ginger biscuits, the good polite Winnie came out and sat in the garden. When my little sister showed her the bluebird tablecloth Winnie only peeped and said, "My mother has a tablecloth with roses and pansies and forget-me-nots on."

And when my mother asked her to have a cake, she said, "No, thank you, bread and butter, please," and she wouldn't have a jam-tart, she had one little ginger biscuit, and then she said she wasn't hungry any more. Wasn't she polite?

My little sister wasn't polite like that. She had four cakes and three jam tarts, and eight ginger biscuits. One, two, three, four, five, six, seven, eight, like that – and she ate them all up.

After tea good polite Winnie's mother came to fetch her home. She took off Winnie's apron and Winnie said,

"Good-bye, and thank you for minding me," in a quiet good voice like that, "Good afternoon," she said.

When she had gone, my mother said, "What a quiet child." But what do you think my funny little sister said? She said, "I'm glad I'm not as good as all that."

And my mother said, "Oh, well, you are not so bad, I suppose."

17 · My naughty little sister is a curly girl

WINNIE, THE LITTLE girl who used to come and see us sometimes when I was a little girl with a naughty little sister, was a very quiet, tidy child. She never rushed about and shouted or played dirty games, and she always wore neat clean dresses.

Winnie had some of those long round and round curls like chimney-pots that hung round her head in a very tidy way, and when Winnie moved her head these little curls jumped up and down. Mother told us that these curls were called ringlets.

One day, when Winnie and her mother were spending the afternoon at our house, my sister sat staring very hard at Winnie's ringlets, and all of a sudden she got up and went over to her and pushed one of her little fingers into one of Winnie's tidy ringlets.

Then, because the ringlet looked so nice on her finger, she pushed another finger into another ringlet.

Now, if anyone had interfered with my sister's hair she

would have screamed and screamed – she even made a fuss when our mother brushed it – but Winnie sat still and quiet in a very mousy way, although I don't think she liked having her hair meddled with any more than my sister would have done.

Winnie's mother certainly didn't like it, and she said in a polite firm voice, "Please don't fiddle with Winifred's hair, dear; the curls may come out."

Then Winnie's mother said to our mother, "They take such ages to put in every night."

When Winnie's mother said this, my funny sister thought that the curls would come right out of Winnie's head if she touched them too much. And she thought that Winnie's mother would have to pick all the curls up and put them back into Winnie's head at night-time. So she stopped touching Winnie's hair at once, and went and sat down again.

She didn't think she would like to be Winnie with falling-out curls.

My little sister sat looking at Winnie though, in case a curl should fall out on its own, but when it didn't, she got tired of looking at her, and went out into the garden instead to talk over the fence to dear Mrs Cocoa Jones.

"Mrs Cocoa," she said, "Winnie has funny curls."

Mrs Cocoa was surprised when my sister said this, so she told her what Winnie's mother had said about the curls coming out.

115

Now, Mrs Cocoa was a kind polite lady and she didn't laugh at my little sister for making such a funny mistake. She just told her all about how Winnie's mother made Winnie's curls for her.

Mrs Cocoa told my sister how, when *she* was a little girl, her kind old grandmother had curled *her* hair. She said that her grandmother had made her hair damp with a wet brush and had twisted her hair up in little pieces of rag, and how she had gone to bed with her hair twisted up like this and how, next morning, when her grandmother had undone her curlers she had had ringlets just like Winnie's.

My sister was very interested to hear all this.

"Of course," Mrs Cocoa said, "my granny only did up my hair on Saturday nights so that it would be curly for Sunday. On ordinary week-nights I had two little pigtails like yours."

When my sister heard Mrs Cocoa saying about how her grandmother curled her hair for her, she began to smile as big as that.

"I know, Mrs Cocoa," she said, "you can make me a curly girl."

Mrs Cocoa said that my sister would have to sit still and not scream then, and my sister said she would be very still indeed, so Mrs Cocoa said, "Well then, if your mother is willing, I'll pop in tonight and put some curlers in for you."

After that, my sister went back into the house, and sat very quietly looking at Winnie and Winnie's beautiful ringlets and smiling in a pussy-cat pleased way to herself.

She didn't say anything to Winnie and her mother about what kind Mrs Cocoa was going to do, but when they had gone she told Mother and me all about it, and Mother said it was very kind of Mrs Cocoa to offer to make ringlets of my sister's hair, and she said, "Mrs Cocoa can try anyway, although I can't think *how* you will sit still without making a fuss."

But my sister said, "I want ringlets like Winnie's," and she said it in a very loud voice to show that she wouldn't fuss, so our mother didn't say anything else; and when Mrs Cocoa came over at my sister's bedtime, with a lot of strips of pink rag, and asked for my sister's hairbrush and a basin of water, our mother fetched them for her without saying a word about how my sister usually fussed.

Now, my sister had said that she wasn't going to be a naughty girl when Mrs Cocoa curled her hair, and she knew that Mother expected her to be naughty and that I expected her to be naughty, so, although she found that she didn't like having her hair twisted up into rags very much, she was good as gold.

My sister didn't like having her hair twisted up into those rags one bit. You see, her hair was rather long, and Mrs Cocoa had to twist and twist very tightly indeed to make sure that the curlers would stay in; and the tighter the curl-rags were the more uncomfortable they felt.

But my sister didn't say so. She sat very good and quiet and she thought about all those lovely Winnie-ringlets, and when Mrs Cocoa had finished she thanked her very nicely indeed and went upstairs with Rosy-primrose, with her hair all curled up tight with little pink rags sticking up all over her head.

But, oh dear.

Have *you* ever tried to sleep with curlers in *your* hair? My sister tried and tried, but wherever she turned her

118

head there was a little knob of hair to lie on and it was most uncomfortable.

She tried to go to sleep with her nose in the pillow but that was most feathery and unpleasant.

In the end the poor child went to sleep with her head

right over the edge of the bed and her arm tight round the bedpost to keep herself from falling out.

That wasn't comfortable either, so she woke up.

When my little sister woke up she shouted because she couldn't remember why she was lying in such a funny way, and our mother had to come in to her.

119

When Mother saw how hard it was for my little sister to sleep with her curlers in, she said perhaps they had better come out, and that made my naughty little sister cry because she did want Winnie-ringlets, until Mother said, "Well, if you want curls don't fuss then," and went back to her own bed.

After that my poor sister slept and woke up and slept and woke up all night, but she didn't shout any more, and when morning came she was sleepy and cross and peepy-eyed.

But when she had had her breakfast, Mrs Cocoa came in to undo the curlers, and my sister cheered up and began to smile.

She sat very still while kind Mrs Cocoa took out the rags and carefully combed each ringlet into shape, and when Mrs Cocoa had finished, and my sister climbed up to see herself in the mirror she smiled like anything.

And I smiled and Mother smiled.

She was a curly girl – curlier than Winnie even, because she had a lot more hair than Winnie had. She had real ringlets that you could push your fingers into!

My sister was a proud girl that day; she sat about in a still quiet way – just like Winnie did, and after dinner she fell fast asleep in her chair.

When my sister woke up she sat for a little while and did a lot of thinking, then she got down from her chair and went round to see Mrs Cocoa.

"Thank you very much, Mrs Cocoa, for making me a curly girl," my sister said, "but I don't think I will be curly any more. It makes me too sleepy to be curly."

"I know why Winnie is so quiet now," my sister said, "it's because she can't sleep for curlers. I think I would rather be me, fast asleep with pigtails."

And Mrs Cocoa said, "That's a very good idea, I think. Anyway who wants *you* to look like that Winnie?"

18 · My naughty little sister at the Fair

WHEN I WAS a little girl, my little sister used to eat all her breakfast up, and all her dinner up, and all her tea up, and all her supper up – every bit.

But one day my naughty little sister wouldn't eat her breakfast. She had cornflakes and an egg, and a piece of bread and butter, and an apple, and a big cup of milk, and she wouldn't eat anything.

She said, "No cornflakes."

Then my mother said, "Well, eat your egg," and she said, "No egg. Nasty egg." She said "Nasty apple," too,

and she spilled her milk all over the table. Wasn't she naughty?

My mother said, "You won't go to the Fair this afternoon if you don't eat it all up." So then my naughty little sister began to eat up her breakfast very quickly. She ate the cornflakes and the egg, but she really couldn't manage the apple, and my mother said, "Well, you ate most of your breakfast so I think we shall let you go to the Fair."

Shall I tell you why my naughty little sister hadn't wanted to eat her breakfast? *She was too excited.* And when my naughty little sister was excited, she was very cross and disobedient.

When the Fair-time came, my big cousin Jane came to fetch us. Then my naughty little sister got so excited that she was crosser than ever. My mother dressed her up in her new best blue dress and her new best blue knickers, and her white shoes and blue socks, but my naughty little sister wouldn't help a bit. And you know what that means.

She went all stiff and stubborn, and she wouldn't put her arms in the arm-holes for herself, and she wouldn't lift up her feet for her shoes, and my mother said, "Very well, they shall go without you." Then my naughty little sister lifted up her feet very quickly. Wasn't she bad?

We went on a bus to the Fair, and when we got there, it was very nice. We saw cows and horses and pigs and sheep and chickens, and lots and lots of people. And there were big swings that went swingy-swing, swingy-swing, and roundabouts that went round and round, round and round. Then my naughty little sister said, "I want a swing! I want a swing!"

But my big cousin Jane said, "No, you are too little for those big swings, but you shall go on the little roundabout."

The little roundabout had wooden horses with real reins, and things to put your feet in, and there were little cars on the roundabout, and a little red fire-engine, and a little train.

First, we watched the roundabout going round and round, and when it went round all the cars and horses went up and down, up and down, and the fire-engine and the train went up and down too. The roundabout played music as it went round.

Then, when it stopped, my big cousin said, "Get on, both of you." There were lots of other children there, and some of them were afraid to go on the roundabout, but my little sister wasn't afraid. She was the first child to go on, and she got on all by herself, without *anyone* lifting her at all. Wasn't she a big girl? And do you know what she did? She got into the seat of the red fire-engine, and rang and rang the bell. "Clonkle! Clonkle! Clonkle!" went the bell, and my little sister laughed and laughed, and when the roundabout went round it played nice music, and my naughty little sister said, "Hurrah. I'm going to put the fire out!"

My little sister had four rides on the roundabout. One, two, three, four rides. And then my big cousin Jane said, "We have spent all our money. We will go and look at the people buying horses."

But my little sister got thoroughly nasty again, and she said, "No horse. Nasty horses. Want roundabout." There, wasn't that bad of her? I'm glad you're not like that.

But my cousin said, "Come along at once," and my naughty little sister had to come, but do you know what she did, while we were looking at the horses? *She ran away*. I said she was a naughty child, you know.

Yes. She ran away, and we couldn't find her anywhere. We looked and looked. We went to the roundabouts and she wasn't there. We went to the swings and she wasn't there. She wasn't at the pig place, or the cow place or the chicken place, or any of the other places. So then my big cousin Jane said, "We must ask a policeman. Because policemen are good to lost children."

We asked a lady if she could tell us where a policeman was, and the lady said, "Go over the road to the police-station."

So my cousin took me over the road to the police-station, and we went into a big door, and through another door, and we saw a policeman sitting without his hat on. And the policeman said, "How do you do, children. Can I help you?" Wasn't that nice of him?

Then my big cousin Jane said, "We have lost a naughty little girl." And she told the nice policeman all about my bad little sister, all about what her name was, and where we had lost her, and what she looked like, and the nice policeman wrote it all down in a big book.

Then the kind policeman said, "No, we haven't a little girl here, but if we find her, we will send her home to you in a big car."

So then my cousin Jane and I went home, and it was a long long walk, because we had spent all our pennies on the roundabout.

When we got home, what do you think? There was my

naughty little sister, sitting at the table, eating her tea. She had got home before us after all. And do you know why that was? It was because a kind policeman had found her and taken her home in his big car.

And do you know, my naughty little sister said she'd never, never run off like that again, because it wasn't nice at all, being lost. She said it made her cry.

But, my naughty little sister said, if she did get lost again, she would find another nice policeman to take her home, because policemen are so kind to lost children.

19 · My naughty little sister does knitting

EVERY SINGLE MORNING, when it was eleven o'clock, Mrs Cocoa Jones used to bang hard on her kitchen wall with the handle of her floor-brush, and as our kitchen was right the other side of the wall, my naughty little sister could hear very well, and would bang and bang back to show that she was quite ready.

Then, my little sister would go into Mrs Cocoa Jones's house to drink cocoa with her. Wasn't that a nice idea?

My little sister used to go in to see Mrs Cocoa Jones so much that Mr Cocoa Jones made a little low gate between his garden and our father's garden so that my little sister could pop in without having to go all round the front of the houses each time. Mr Cocoa Jones made a nice little archway over the gate, and planted a little rose-tree to climb over it, especially for her. Wasn't she a fortunate child? So you see, Mrs Cocoa Jones was a very great friend.

Well now, Mrs Cocoa Jones was a lady who was always knitting and knitting, and as she hadn't any little boys and girls of her own, she used to knit a lot of lovely woollies for my naughty little sister, and for me.

She knitted us red jumpers and blue jumpers, and yellow jumpers and red caps and blue caps and yellow caps to match, and she also knitted a blue jumper for Rosy-primrose, who was my naughty little sister's favourite doll, and when she had finished all the caps and jumpers, she made us lots of pairs of socks. So, every time we saw Mrs Cocoa, she always had a bag of wool and a lot of clicky needles.

Sometimes, when Mrs Cocoa Jones wanted the wool wound up, she would ask my naughty little sister to hold it for her, and that fidgety child would drop it and tangle it, until Mr Cocoa Jones used to say "It looks to me as if you will be doing knotting not knitting with that lot," to Mrs Cocoa. And my funny little sister laughed because she thought it very funny to say "knotting" like that.

Now, one day Mrs Cocoa Jones said, "Would you like to learn to knit?" to my naughty little sister.

"Would you like to learn to knit?" she asked my little sister, and my little sister said, "Not very much."

Then Mrs Cocoa said, "Well, but think of all the nice things you could make for everyone. You could knit Christmas presents and birthday presents all by yourself."

Then my naughty little sister thought it would be rather nice to learn to knit, so she said, "All right then, Mrs Cocoa Jones, would you please teach me?" So Mrs Cocoa Jones

lent her a pair of rather bendy needles and she gave her
some wool, and she showed her how to knit.

So, carefully, carefully my little sister learned to put the
wool round the needle, and carefully, carefully to bring it
out and make a stitch, and carefully, carefully to make
another until she could really truly knit.

Then my naughty little sister was very pleased, because

she had a good idea. She thought that as Mr Cocoa Jones
had made her such a nice little gate, she would knit him a
new scarf for his birthday, because his old scarf had got all
moth-holey. The naughty little baby moths had eaten bits

of scarf and made holes in it, so my little sister thought he would like a new one very much.

She didn't tell anyone about it. Not even Mrs Cocoa Jones: she wanted it to be a real secret.

Well now, Mrs Cocoa had given my little sister all her odds and endsy bits of wool, the red bits and the blue bits and the yellow bits from our jumpers, and some grey and purple and white and black and brown bits as well, so my little sister thought she would make a beautiful scarf.

She went secretly, secretly into corners to knit this beautiful scarf for Mr Cocoa Jones's birthday.

She kept it carefully hidden all the time she wasn't making it. She hid it in lots of funny places too. She hid it under her pillow, and in the coal-shed and behind the settee, and in the flour-tub. But most of the time she was knitting and knitting to have it made in time. So that, when Mr Cocoa Jones's birthday did come, it was quite ready and quite finished.

It was a very pretty scarf because of all the pretty colours my little sister had used, and although it was a bit coaly and a bit floury here and there, it still looked very lovely, and Mr Cocoa Jones was very pleased with it.

He said, "It's the best scarf I have ever had!"

Then my little sister told him all about how she had knitted it, and she showed him some holes in it too, where the stitches had dropped, and Mr Cocoa Jones said they would make nice homes for the baby moths to live in anyway, so my little sister was glad she had dropped the stitches.

Then Mr Cocoa Jones said that as it was the very nicest scarf he had ever had knitted for him, it would be a shame to waste it by wearing it every day. So he said he would get

Mrs Cocoa to put it away for him for High Days and Holidays.

So Mrs Cocoa wrapped it up very neatly and nicely in blue laundry paper, and she let my little sister put it away in Mr Cocoa's drawer for him, and Mr Cocoa wore his old scarf for every day until Mrs Cocoa had time to knit him another one.

20 · When my naughty little sister wasn't well

I HOPE YOU aren't a shy child. My naughty little sister wasn't shy, but she used to pretend to be sometimes, and when nice aunts and uncles came to see us, she wouldn't say, "How do you do?" or shake hands or anything; and if they tried to talk to her she would run off down the garden and hide among the currant bushes until they went away.

But my naughty little sister talked and talked when she wanted to. She talked to the milkman and the baker and the coalman and the window-cleaner man, and all the other people who came to the door, and when they came she got terribly in their way, because she talked to them so much, but they all liked my naughty little sister.

One day she upset all the milkman's bottles, and he only said, "Never mind, no use crying over spilt milk," and another day she shut the cellar up just as the coalman was going to tip the coal in, and he only said, "Well, well now, there's a job for your father!" and she climbed up the ladder after the window-cleaning man and then she cried because she was afraid to come down, but *he* only said, "There! There! Don't cry, dearie," and he lent her his leathery thing to wipe her tears on.

So you see, they liked my naughty little sister very much, but wasn't she naughty?

Well now, one day my poor naughty little sister wasn't very well. She sat in her chair and looked very miserable and said, "I'm not a very well girl today."

So my mother said, "You shall go to bed and have a hot drink and a hot-water bottle, and we shall send for the doctor to come and see what's wrong with you."

And my naughty little sister said, "No doctor! Nasty doctor!" Wasn't she a silly cuckoo? Fancy saying "No doctor" when she wasn't well!

But my mother said, "He's a nice doctor. You must tell him how you feel, and then he will make you all better."

Then my naughty little sister said, "I'm too shy. I won't talk to him." She said it in a cross, growly voice, "I *won't* talk to him!"

So my naughty little sister went to bed, and she had a hot-water bottle and a hot drink. Also, she had her best books, and all her dolls and her teddy-bears, but she felt so not-well that she didn't want any of these things at all.

Presently my naughty little sister heard a knock at the front door, and she said, "No doctor," and hid her face under the sheet.

But it wasn't the doctor, it was the nice milkman, and when he heard my naughty little sister wasn't well, he sent her his love, and a note-book with lines on, and a blue pencil to write with.

Then my naughty little sister heard the front door again, and she said, "No doctor," again, and hid her face again, but it was the nice baker, and he sent my naughty little sister *his* love and a little spongy cake in case she fancied it.

Then she heard the front door again, and she said, "No doctor – nasty doctor," but it was the nice coalman, and

he sent my naughty little sister *his* love and a red rose from his cap that smelt rosy and coaly.

After that my naughty little sister began to feel a much happier girl, and she didn't hide her face any more, so that when the window-cleaner man came to clean the window, she could see him smiling through the glass, and when he popped his head in and asked, "How's the invalid?" my naughty little sister said, "I'm not a well girl today."

The window-cleaner man said, "Well, the doctor will soon put you right."

And my naughty little sister watched the window-cleaner man rubbing away with the leathery thing, and then she said, "No doctor," to the window-cleaner man, "No doctor," she said, out loud.

"Yes doctor," said the window-cleaner man.

"No doctor," said my naughty little sister.

"That's a silly idea you've got," said the window-cleaner man. "The doctor will make you a well girl again."

Then my naughty little sister began to cry and cry. "No doctor, no doctor. I'm too shy." Like that, in that miserable way.

And then the window-cleaner man said, "What a pity you won't have the doctor, because you won't see his listening-thing, or his glass-stick-thing to pop under your tongue, or the doctor's bag that he keeps his little bottles in."

Then my naughty little sister stopped crying and said, "What listening-thing? What stick-thing?"

"Ah," said the window-cleaning man, "I shan't tell you that. Why should I? But it's a pity you won't see that doctor and find out for yourself." That's what the window-cleaner man said.

Then the window-cleaner man went away, and took his ladder with him, and my naughty little sister stayed in her bed and thought and thought.

And presently, when she heard a knock at the front door, my naughty little sister didn't say, "No doctor," and hide her face under the sheet, even though it really *was* the doctor this time. She didn't do anything silly like that at all.

My naughty little sister waited and waited until she heard my mother coming upstairs with the doctor, and when the doctor came into her bedroom my naughty little sister didn't say, "Go away," or pretend to be shy, or scream, or do any of the bad things she could do.

She said, "Hallo, doctor," and then the doctor said, "Hallo, and how are you today?" and my naughty little sister said, "I'm not a well girl today."

Then she said, "Have you got your doctor's bag, and your listening-thing, and your glass-stick-thing to pop into my mouth?" and the doctor said, "Yes, I have."

Then my naughty little sister was pleased as pleased, and she liked the doctor so much after all, that she took all the medicine he sent her without being cross once, and got a well girl again very quickly.

21 · Going fishing

ONE DAY SOME children came to our house and asked my mother if I could go fishing with them.

They had jam-jars with string on them, and fishing-nets and sandwiches and lemonade.

My mother said "Yes" – I could go with them; and she found *me* a jam-jar and a fishing-net, and cut *me* some sandwiches.

Then my naughty little sister said, "I want to go! I want to go!" Just like that. So my mother said I might as well take her too.

Then my mother cut some sandwiches for my little sister, but she didn't give her a jam-jar or a fishing-net because she said she was too little to go near the water. My mother gave my little sister a basket to put stones in, because my little sister liked to pick up stones, and she gave me a big bottle of lemonade to carry for both of us.

My mother said, "You mustn't let your little sister get herself wet. You must keep her away from the water." And I said, "All right, Mother, I promise."

So then we went off to the little river, and we took our

shoes off and our socks off, and tucked up our clothes, and we went into the water to catch fish with our fishing-nets, and we filled our jam-jars with water to put the fishes in when we caught them. And we said to my naughty little sister, "You mustn't come, you'll get yourself wet."

Well, we paddled and paddled and fished and fished, but we didn't catch any fish at all, not one little tiny one even. Then a boy said, "Look, there is your little sister in the water too!"

And, do you know, my naughty little sister had walked right into the water with her shoes and socks on, and she was trying to fish with her little basket.

I said, "Get out of the water," and she said, "No."

I said, "Get out *at once*," and she said, "I don't want to."

I said, "You'll get all wet," and she said, "I don't care." Wasn't she naughty?

So I said, "I must fetch you out then," and my naughty little sister tried to run away in the water. Which is a silly thing to do because she fell down and got all wet.

She got her frock wet, and her petticoat wet, and her knickers wet, and her vest wet, and her hair wet, and her hair-ribbons – all soaking wet. Of course, I told you her shoes and socks were wet before.

And she cried and cried.

So we fetched her out of the water, and we said, "Oh, dear, she will catch a cold," and we took off all her wet things: her wet frock, and her wet petticoat and her wet knickers and her wet vest, and her wet hair-ribbons, *and* her wet shoes and socks, and we hung all the things to dry on the bushes in the sunshine, and we wrapped my naughty little sister up in a woolly cardigan.

My little sister cried and cried. So we gave her the sandwiches, and she ate them all up. She ate up her sandwiches and my sandwiches, and the other children's sandwiches all up – and she cried and cried.

Then we gave her the lemonade and she spilled it all over the grass, and she cried and cried.

Then one of the children gave her an apple, and another of the children gave her some toffees, and, while she was eating these, we took her clothes off the bushes and ran about with them in the sunshine until they were dry. When her clothes were quite dry, we put them all back on her again, and she screamed and screamed because she didn't want her clothes on any more.

So, I took her home, and my mother said, "Oh, you've let your little sister fall into the water."

And I said, "How do you know? Because we dried all her clothes," and my mother said, "Ah, but you didn't *iron* them." My little sister's clothes were all crumpled and messy.

Then my mother said I should not have any sugary biscuits for supper because I was disobedient. Only bread and butter, and she said my little sister must go straight to bed, and have some hot milk to drink.

And my mother said to my little sister, "Don't you think you were a naughty little girl to go in the water?"

And my naughty little sister said, "I won't do it any more, because it was too wet."

But, do you know, when my mother went to throw away the stones out of my little sister's basket, she found a little fish in the bottom, which my naughty little sister had caught!

22 · My naughty little sister cuts out

ONCE, WHEN I was a little girl, and my naughty little sister was a very little girl, it rained and rained and rained. It rained every day, and it rained all the time, and everything got wetter and wetter and wetter, and when my naughty little sister went out she had to wear her mackintosh and her wellingtons.

My naughty little sister had a beautiful red mackintosh-cape with a hood – just like Little Red Riding Hood's – and she had a little red umbrella. My little sister used to carry her umbrella under her cape, because she didn't want it to get wet. Wasn't she a silly girl?

When my naughty little sister went down the road, the rain went plop, plop, plop, plop, on to her head, and scatter-scatter-scatter against her cape, and trickle, trickle down her cheeks, and her wellington boots went splish-splosh, splish-splosh in the puddles.

My naughty little sister liked puddles very much, and she splished and sploshed such a lot that the water got into the tops of her wellingtons and made her feet wet inside, and then my naughty little sister was very sorry, because she caught a cold.

She got a nasty, sneezy, atishoo-y cold, and couldn't go out in the rain any more. My poor little sister looked very miserable when my mother said she could not go out. But her cold was very bad, and she had a red nose, and red eyes, and a nasty buzzy ear – all because of getting her feet wet, and every now and again – she couldn't help it – she said, "A-a-tishoo!"

Now, my naughty little sister was a fidgety child. She wouldn't sit down quietly to hear a story like you do, or play nicely with a toy, or draw pictures with a pencil – she just fidgeted and wriggled and grumbled all the time, and said, "Want to go out in the rain – want to splash and splash," in the crossest and growliest voice, and then she said, "A-a-tishoo!" even when she didn't want to, because of the nasty cold she'd got. And she grumbled and grumbled and grumbled.

My mother made her orange-drink, but she grumbled. My mother gave her cough-stuff, but she grumbled, and really no one knew how to make her good.

My mother said, "Why don't you look at a picture-book?"

And my naughty little sister said, "No book, nasty book."

Then my mother said, "Well, would you like to play with my button-box?" and my naughty little sister said she thought she might like that. But when she had dropped all the buttons out and spilled them all over the floor, she said, "No buttons, tired of buttons. A-a-tishoo!" She said, "A-a-tishoo" like that, because she couldn't help it.

My mother said, "Dear me, what can I do for the child?"

Then my mother had a good idea. She said, "I know, you can make a scrap-book!"

So my mother found a big book with clean pages, and a lot of old birthday cards and Christmas cards, and some old picture-books, and a big pot of sticky paste and she showed my naughty little sister how to make a scrap-book.

My naughty little sister was quite pleased, because she had never been allowed to use scissors before, and these were the nice snippy ones from mother's work-box.

My naughty little sister cut out a picture of a cow, and

a basket with roses in, and a lady in a red dress, and a house and a squirrel, and she stuck them all in the big book with the sticky paste, and then she laughed and laughed.

Do you know why she laughed? She laughed because she had stuck them all in the book in a funny way. She stuck the lady in first, and then she put the basket of roses on the lady's head, and the cow on top of that, and then she put the house and the squirrel under the lady's feet. My naughty little sister thought that the lady looked very funny with the basket of flowers and the cow on her head.

So my naughty little sister amused herself for quite a long while, and my mother said, "Thank goodness," and went upstairs to tidy the bedrooms, as my naughty little sister wasn't grumbling any more.

But that naughty child soon got tired of the scrap-book, and when she got tired of it, she started rubbing the sticky paste over the table, and made the table all gummy. Wasn't that nasty of her?

Then she poked the scissors into the birthday cards and the Christmas cards, and made them look very ugly, and then, because she liked to do snip-snipping with the scissors, she looked round for something big to cut.

Fancy looking round for mischief like that! But she did. She didn't care at all, she just looked round for something to cut.

She snipped up all father's newspaper with the scissors,

and she tried to snip the pussy-cat's tail, only pussy put her back up and said "Pss", and frightened my naughty little sister.

So my naughty little sister looked round for something that she could cut up easily, and she found a big brown-paper parcel on a chair – a parcel all tied up with white string.

My naughty sister was so bad because she couldn't go out and play in the wet that she cut the string of the parcel. She knew that she shouldn't, but she didn't care a bit. She cut the string right through, and pulled it all off. She did that because she thought it would be nice to cut up all the brown paper that was round the parcel.

So she dragged the parcel on to the floor, and began to pull off the brown paper. But when the brown paper was off, my very naughty little sister found something inside that she thought would be much nicer to cut. It was a lovely piece of silky, rustly material with little flowers all over it – the sort of special stuff that party-dresses are made of.

Now my naughty little sister knew that she mustn't cut stuff like that, but she didn't care. She thought she would just make a quick snip to see how it sounded when it was cut. So she did make a snip, and the stuff went "scc-scrr-scrr" as the scissors bit it, and my naughty little sister was so pleased that she forgot about everything else, and just cut and cut.

And then, all of a sudden . . . yes!

In came my mother!

My mother was cross when she saw the sticky table, and the cut-up newspaper, but when she looked on the floor and saw my naughty little sister cutting the silky stuff, she was very, very angry.

"You are a bad, bad child," my mother said. "You shall not have the scissors any more. Your kind Aunt Betty is going to be married soon, and she sent this nice stuff for me to make you a bridesmaid's dress, because she wanted you to hold up her dress in church for her. Now you won't be able to go."

My naughty little sister cried and cried because she wanted to be a bridesmaid and because she liked to have new dresses very much. But it was no use, because the stuff was all cut up.

After that my naughty little sister tried to be a good girl until her cold was better.

23 · My naughty little sister goes to school

ONE DAY, MY mother had a letter from my granny, to say that she was ill in bed, and would Mother come over for a day to see her?

So my mother wrote a letter to my school-teacher to ask if my little sister could come to school with me next day, as granny was ill. My teacher said, "Yes, she can come if she will be good." And wasn't my funny little sister pleased!

Do you know what she did? She found an old case belonging to my father, and she put in it all the things she thought she would want for school next day. She put in a pencil and a rubber, and some crayons and some story-books, and an apple and a matchbox, and Rosy-primrose who was her doll.

Then she went to bed very quickly like a good girl. She didn't splash about in the bath, or scream when she had her hair done, or grumble about her supper, or say her prayers naughtily, or worry and worry for lots of stories in bed. No. She shut her eyes quickly so as to go to sleep and make tomorrow come as soon as soon. That's what the sensible child did.

And in the morning, she got up early, and she *dressed herself*. Yes! Even the *buttons*, and her socks! To show the teacher how nicely she could do it. Then, while our mother was getting the breakfast ready, she went out into the garden and she picked a nice bunch of flowers out of her own garden for the teacher. So for once in a while she was my good little sister.

Well now, when my little sister got to school, she was still being very good. She said, "Good morning," to everyone and she came nicely into school, and because she looked so good and special the teacher said she could sit next to me all day.

So my little sister sat down right next to me, and stared and stared at all the other children in the room, and when she saw them opening their bags and cases and getting out their books and pencil-boxes, she opened her case and took out all her things too. She took out the pencil and the rubber, and the crayons and the story-books but she left the apple and the matchbox and Rosy-primrose in the case because she wanted them for play-time.

When school started, my little sister stood up very straight to sing the school hymns, and she shut her eyes very tight for the school prayers, and then she sat down as good as good, nice and straight like the teacher told us to.

Then the teacher called all the children's names, and

when each child's name was called, the child said, "Present." My naughty little sister was very surprised, and when my name was called I said, "Present," too. But the teacher didn't call my little sister's name, because she wasn't a real schoolchild, and do you know what my naughty little sister did?

She forgot to be a good child, and she started to shout, "I want a present, I want a present." Wasn't she silly?

But after that my little sister was very good again, and the teacher let her play with some plasticine. My little sister made a red basket with the plasticine, and the teacher said it was very good, and put it on the mantelpiece for everyone to see.

Then our teacher read us a story, and my little sister was very interested, and when our teacher asked questions about the story, and all the children put their hands up, my little sister put her hand up too, and all the children laughed. But our teacher said they mustn't laugh, and she asked my little sister a real big-child's question about the story, and my little sister gave the right answer. Then our teacher said, as my little sister was such a clever child she could have ten out of ten. (You know ten out of ten is a very big thing to have at school.)

So our teacher wrote "Ten out of ten" on a piece of paper for my little sister and put it on the mantelpiece for her with the plasticine basket, and my little sister was a very proud child.

When dinner-time came, our teacher let my little sister sit with her, and my little sister was so good that the teacher said all the other children should try to be like her. Wasn't she behaving well?

In the afternoon we all drew pictures with our crayons, and my little sister drew a picture with her crayons. She was very pleased to think she had brought her own crayons to school.

I drew a little house, and a tree and a pond, and some little people. But do you know what my little sister drew? She drew the teacher, and all the school-children! Yes, all of them in the class. The teacher was very pleased to see such a lovely drawing, because my little sister had not forgotten anything – she had even put in her plasticine basket and her ten out of ten writing. So Teacher said the drawing must go on the mantelpiece with the other clever

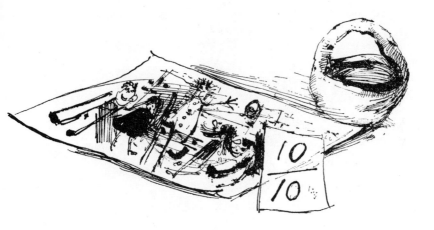

things. My little sister drew in her drawing very small next to the plasticine basket, and then the picture was put up for everyone to see.

Then we all went out into the playground and did drill, and my little sister did drill as well, and she stood so straight, and put her arms so nicely that Teacher let her do it in front of all the class.

So you see, she was being a very good child.

When we went back into school though, and did reading, my little sister got very quiet, and very still, and do you know what happened? She fell fast asleep in the desk.

She slept and slept right until our mother came to fetch us home, and, because she had been so good and no trouble, our teacher let her take home the lovely drawing, and the plasticine basket, and the ten out of ten paper.

24 · The Cocoa week-end

WHEN I WAS a little girl I sometimes went to stay with my godmother-aunt in the country, for the week-end.

My mother would pack a little case for me, and then my godmother would come to spend a day with us and take me back with her.

My little sister was always very interested when she saw Mother packing my case, and she would remember things to go in it, and go and fetch them without being asked.

She used to ask me questions and questions about going visiting, and when I had told her everything she used to ask me all over again because she liked hearing it so much.

I told her about the nice little blue bed that I slept in at my godmother's and the picture of the big dog and the little dog on the bedroom wall. I told her and told her about them.

Then she wanted to hear about the things we had to eat and the things I did. I told her about all the tiny little baby-looking cakes that my godmother made, and about my godmother's piano, and how she let me play little made-up tunes on it if I wanted to.

And she would say, "Tell me again about the piano," my little sister would say, "Tell me again. I like about the piano."

So I would tell her about the piano all over again, and then I would pretend to play tunes on the table, and my sister would pretend to play tunes on the table too, and we would laugh and laugh.

But, when my mother said, "Wouldn't you like to go on a visit one day?" my little sister would say, "I'm not sure."

My little sister told her friend Mrs Cocoa all about my goings away, and Mrs Cocoa was surprised to find how much my little sister knew about it, and *she* said, "Wouldn't you like to go on a visit one day?" as well.

When Mrs Cocoa said this, my sister said, "I don't think I should mind the visit but I shouldn't like the long-way-away."

My little sister said, "I should like to sleep in a different bed with a different picture on the wall and eat different dinners and play the piano, but I don't think I should like to go a long way to do it."

You see my godmother-aunt did live quite a long way from our house, and my little sister was rather frightened to think what a long way it was.

Now kind Mrs Cocoa thought about what my little sister had said, and the next time she heard that I was going to stay with my godmother-aunt, she said to my little sister, "How would you like to go away for a week-

158

end, too? How would you like to come and stay with me?"

Mrs Cocoa said, "You can sleep in my little spare bed-room and eat all your dinners and things with Mr Cocoa and me, and you won't be a long-way-away, will you?"

Wasn't that a lovely idea for clever Mrs Cocoa to have had? Mrs Cocoa lived next door to us, and my little sister knew her house very well, but she had never slept there and had all her dinners and things there, so it would be a real visit, wouldn't it?

My sister was very pleased. It was just what she wanted: a real visit that was not far away, so she said at once, "Please, Mrs Cocoa, I should like that."

So when my mother packed my case she packed one for my naughty little sister as well, and my little sister helped her to fetch things for both the cases.

When my godmother-aunt was ready to go, and I put my best hat and coat on, my sister said she must put *her* best hat and coat on too because she was going visiting just like her big sister.

Now you know there was a little gate that Mr Cocoa had made in the fence between his garden and ours, especially for my little sister so that she could come in to see Mrs Cocoa when she wanted to. It was a dear little gate and my little sister was always using it, but because she was going to visit Mrs Cocoa, she said she didn't want to go through her gate, she wanted to go through Mrs Cocoa's *front door*.

"I'm not Mrs Cocoa's next-door girl," she said; "I'm a visitor!"

So my father carried the case for her, and my little

sister went down our front garden and through our front gate and through Mrs Cocoa's front gate and *up* her front garden and Father lifted her up so that she could knock on Mrs Cocoa's knocker.

My little sister knocked very hard and called out, "Here I am, Mrs Cocoa; I've come to visit you!" And Mrs Cocoa opened the door, and said, "Well, I *am* pleased to see you come in, do. You're just in time for tea."

"Come in, my dear," Mrs Cocoa said, and Mr Cocoa came out into the hall and said, "I'll take your luggage, ma'am," just as if he hardly knew my sister at all! Wasn't that nice?

My little sister said, "Thank you, Mr Jones." Not "Mr Cocoa". She said, "Thank you, *Mr Jones*," in a visitor-way.

Then she kissed our father "good-bye" and Father said, "Have a good time, old lady," and then she was really on a visit by herself.

Mrs Cocoa gave my sister a very beautiful tea with all her best moss-rose tea-set on the table too, and that was exciting because although my sister had known Mrs Cocoa a long time she had never seen the moss-rose tea-set used before.

Then Mrs Cocoa took my sister upstairs to show her where she was going to sleep, and that was exciting too, because Mrs Cocoa had found a bed-cover with flowers and dragons and gold curly things needleworked all over it, that my little sister had never seen before and this was on the little bed she was to sleep in.

There was a new picture on the wall too. Mrs Cocoa had told Mr Cocoa about the picture at my godmother-aunt's house, and kind Mr Cocoa had found a picture in a book and put it in a frame specially for the Visit. It was a picture of a singing lady lying in some water with flowers floating on it. Mr Cocoa said he liked the picture because the flowers and bushes and things in it looked so real.

My little sister liked the picture too. She said she liked it because the naughty lady hadn't taken her dress off, and she was wet as wet. She liked to have a picture of a naughty wet lady to look at, she said.

Weren't the Cocoas kind to think of all these nice surprises? Mr Cocoa said, "We haven't got a piano, but I've got something else here that ought to keep you out of mischief."

And do you know what he had? It was a musical-box! It was a little brown box with a glass window in the top, and at the side of the box there was a key. When you turned the key a little shiny thing with holes in it went round and round – you could see it through the glass window, and a pretty little tune came out of the box that Mr Cocoa said was called "The Bluebells of Scotland".

If you want to know what it sounded like perhaps you can ask someone to hum it for you.

Mr Cocoa showed my sister how to wind the musical-box and then he said she could play it whenever she liked. And she did play it – lots and lots of times while she was visiting.

My sister stayed with the dear Cocoa Joneses all that week-end and had a lovely time with them. She slept in the little bed and ate Mrs Cocoa's dinners and things and played the musical-box and went for walks with Mr

Cocoa while Mrs Cocoa had a rest, and it was all very
strange and pleasant.

But, do you know, my little sister never once came back
home! She never even knocked on the wall to our mother!
Not once. Mother said she saw my little sister playing in
Mrs Cocoa's garden, and she watched her going off for
walks, but my little sister didn't even look at our house!

She was really being away on a visit.

When the week-end was over, Mrs Cocoa packed her

case for her, and Mr Cocoa took her home by the front door to show that she had been away.

When my little sister saw me again, she didn't ask about *my* visit – oh no! She told me instead all about her visit to the Cocoas. She told me about the dragon and flower bed-cover, and the naughty lady picture, and she said, "There wasn't a piano, but I played another thing."

My little sister couldn't remember the name of the musical-box though, so she said, "I played a la-la box," and she la-la'd all the "Bluebells of Scotland" tune for me without making one mistake. Wasn't she clever!

25 · My naughty little sister and the guard

DO YOU LIKE trains?

When I was a little girl I didn't like trains at all; but my little sister did. I thought that trains were horrid and noisy and puffy and steamy, but my little sister said they were lovely things, and when she saw one she waved and waved and shouted and shouted to it.

Well now, one day a kind aunt wrote to our mother to ask if my little sister would like to go and stay for a week-end. All by herself. Not with my father or mother, or even with me, but all by herself like a grown-up lady!

My mother said, "I don't think she's old enough," and my father said, "I don't think she's good enough," and I said, "She'll be too frightened." Because, if you remember, she *had* been frightened about visiting people.

But my little sister said, "I should like to go and stay for a week-end all by myself. I *am* an old enough girl, and I am not a frightened girl any more. I want to go!"

My mother didn't say anything and my father didn't

say anything and I didn't say anything, and my little sister knew why that was, because she said, "I'm not a good girl now, but I will be good as gold if you let me go."

So my father and mother said they thought she might go if she *was* as good as gold. So my little sister was good. She was quiet and tidy and whispery all the week and when the week-end came she *did* go away. All on her own.

This is the exciting thing that happened to her.

Our kind aunt lived quite a long way away, and my little sister had to go on a train *all by herself*.

Wasn't that exciting? All by herself. She had a little brown case with her nightdress inside, and her slippers and her dressing-gown and her best dress for Sunday and all the things she had taken to dear Mrs Cocoa's. My little sister carried Rosy-primrose under her arm, but of course Mother carried the case to the station for her.

"Auntie will meet you at the other end," Mother said. "So she will carry it to her house for you."

"I hope Auntie won't forget to look for me," said my little sister, "because I don't think I could open a train door all by myself."

"That's all right," our mother told her. "I'm going to ask the guard to keep an eye on you."

My little sister was going to say "What guard?" and ask questions and questions, but she knew that Mother was in a hurry to get the ticket. When she got to the station she was very excited. She *wanted* to fidget and climb on

166

all the parcels and run along the platform and peep at the
man who puts the parcels on the weighing machine. But
she didn't. She remembered about being good as gold.
Wasn't she sensible?

When the train came in, she didn't rush about or fuss;

she walked nicely down the platform beside Mother to
where the guard was standing, and when Mother stopped
to speak to the guard my little sister didn't talk at all. She
just stared because the guard was such a big, beautiful man.

The guard had a big, red, beautiful face and a big,
fluffy, black moustache and a golden glittery band on his
cap and a silver glittery whistle round his neck and two

beautiful flags – a red one and a green one under his arm.

"I am going to put this little girl in the end carriage, Guard," our mother said, "and I wonder if you would be kind enough to look after her ticket for her, and see that she gets off at the right station?"

The guard smiled very kindly then at my little sister. "She is a very little girl," he said. "Is she a good child? If she is, she can come in the guard's van with me for the journey."

My little sister thought she had better say something, because she thought how nice it would be to travel in a real guard's van with a real guard, almost as nice as travelling with the engine-driver and not nearly so hot and coaly. She said, "I am not always a good child. But I am being very good this week."

So the guard said, "That's good enough for me. In you go then," and my sister climbed up into the guard's van.

He said, "Sit on my little seat in the corner there." And although it was rather a high little seat my little sister managed to climb on to it while the guard put her little case into the van, and picked up some parcels from the platform and put them in too.

Then the guard took his green flag, and blew his whistle, and Mother called out, "Good-bye, give my love to Auntie," and the train started to move. The guard jumped in quickly and shut the door. And they were off!

What a very nice man the guard was! He talked all the

time to my little sister. He showed her a lantern that made red and green lights, and let her look at some sheets of paper with lines and printing on them that he said he had to write on every day. He lent my sister a pencil and let her scribble on the back of one of his pieces of paper, but it was very difficult because the train was so bumpy, so he gave her an apple to eat instead.

Each time the train stopped at a station the guard jumped down and took in parcels and sacks and put other parcels and sacks on to the platform. Sometimes there were railway porters waiting for the van, with trucks full of luggage, and they stared at my sister and asked the guard who she was. "Oh, she's my new Mate," the guard said, and my little sister felt proud as proud.

At one station the guard took in a big basket full of chickens, all looking out in a very pecky way. But the guard told my sister they wouldn't really hurt anyone. "I often bring chickens," he said, "and ducks and dogs and cats."

He said that one day he took a very growly dog that grumbled all the time. "I was glad to see the back of him," the guard said.

Then he said, "Yes, I've looked after a lot of animals since I've been on the Line, but you are the first little girl."

My little sister liked to think that she was the first little girl to travel with the guard, and she said, "If you have any other little girls to mind you'll be able to tell them about me." And the guard said that he certainly would.

At last they came to the station that was near our aunt's house, and there was Auntie herself and two of our cousins as well, all waiting for her, and all so happy to see my little sister.

"There's Auntie!" my sister said, and she jumped up and down with excitement as the guard began to open the door.

But she remembered to be a polite child even though she was excited, and before she went off she shook hands with the guard and said, "Thank you for having me" – just like a party – "Thank you for having me."

And the guard said, "It has been a real pleasure," and when the train moved off again, he stayed by his window so as to wave to my little sister and she waved to him. How our cousins stared to see a guard waving from his guard's van window at my little sister.

So my little sister stayed with our auntie for a week-end and she wasn't naughty once. On Monday when she came back home Auntie came with her, because she wanted to come up for the day to see our mother, so my sister didn't travel in the guard's van that time; but she remembered all about it, and when she and Bad Harry played trains in the garden she said, "I must be the guard because I know all about it."

And she did, didn't she?

26 · My naughty little sister and the workmen

MY NAUGHTY LITTLE sister was a very, very inquisitive child. She was always looking and peeping into things that didn't belong to her. She used to open other people's cupboards and boxes just to find out what was inside.

Aren't you glad you aren't inquisitive like that?

Well now, one day a lot of workmen came to dig up all the roads near our house, and my little sister was very interested in them. They were very nice men, but some of them had rather loud shouty voices sometimes. There were shovelling men, and picking men, and men with jumping-about things that went, "Ah-ah-ah-ah-ah-ah-aha-aaa," and men who drank tea out of jam-pots, and men who cooked sausages over fires, and there was an old, old man who sat up all night when the other men had gone home, and who had lots of coats and scarves to keep him warm.

There were lots of things for my little inquisitive sister to see: there were heaps of earth, and red lanterns for the old, old man to light at night-time, and long pole-y things to keep people from falling down the holes in the road, and workmen's huts, and many other things.

When the workmen were in our road, my little sister

used to watch them every day. She used to lean over the gate and stare and stare, but when they went off to the next road she didn't see so much of them.

Well now, I will tell you about the inquisitive thing my naughty little sister did one day, shall I?

Yes. Well, do you remember Bad Harry who was my little sister's best boy-friend? Do you? I thought you did. Now this Bad Harry came one day to ask my mother if my little sister could go round to his house to play with him, and as Bad Harry's house wasn't far away, and as there were no roads to cross, my mother said my little sister could go.

So my little sister put on her hat and her coat, and her scarf and her gloves, because it was a cold nasty day, and went off with her best boy-friend to play with him.

They hurried along like good children until they came to the workmen in the next road, and then they went slow as slow, because there were so many things to see. They looked at this, and at that, and when they got past the workmen they found a very curious thing.

By the road there was a tall hedge, and under the tall hedge there was a mackintoshy bundle.

Now this mackintoshy bundle hadn't anything to do with Bad Harry, and it hadn't anything to do with my naughty little sister; yet do you know they were so inquisitive that they stopped and looked at it.

They had such a good look at it that they had to get right under the hedge to see, and when they got very near it they found it was an old mackintosh wrapped round something or other inside.

Weren't they naughty? They should have gone straight home to Bad Harry's mother's house, shouldn't they? But they didn't. They stayed and looked at the mackintoshy bundle.

And they opened it. They really truly did. It wasn't their bundle, but they opened it wide under the hedge, and do you know what was inside it? I know you aren't an inquisitive meddlesome child, but would you like to know?

Well, inside the bundle there were lots and lots of parcels and packages tied up in red handkerchiefs, and brown paper, and newspaper, and instead of putting them back again like nice children, those little horrors started to open all

174

those parcels, and inside those parcels there were lots of things to eat!

There were sandwiches, and cakes and meat-pies and cold cooked fish, and eggs, and goodness knows what-all.

Weren't those bad children surprised? They couldn't think how all those sandwiches and things could have got into that old mackintosh.

Then Bad Harry said, "Shall we eat some?" You remember he was a greedy lad. But my little sister said, "No, it's picked-up food." My little sister knew that my mother had told her never, never to eat picked-up food. You see she was good about *that*.

Only she was very bad after, because she said, "I know, let's play with it."

So they took out all those sandwiches and cakes, and meat-pies and cold cooked fish and eggs, and they laid them out across the path and made them into pretty patterns on the ground. Then Bad Harry threw a sandwich at my little sister and she threw a meat-pie at him, and they began to have a lovely game.

And then, do you know what happened? A big roary voice called out, "What are you doing with our dinners, you monkeys – you?" And there was a big workman coming towards them, looking so cross and angry that those two bad children screamed and screamed, and because the workman was so roary they turned and ran and ran back down the road, and the big workman ran after them as cross as cross. Weren't they frightened?

When they got back to where the other roadmen were digging, those children were more frightened than ever, because the big workman shouted to all the other workmen all about what those naughty children had done with their dinners.

Yes, those poor workmen had put all their dinners under the hedge in the old mackintosh to keep them dry and safe until dinner-time. As well as being frightened, Bad Harry and my naughty little sister were very ashamed.

They were so ashamed that they did a most silly thing. When they heard the big workman telling the others about their dinners, those silly children ran and hid themselves in one of the pipes that the workmen were putting in the road.

My naughty little sister went first, and old Bad Harry after her. Because my naughty little sister was so frightened

she wriggled in and in the pipe, and Bad Harry came wriggling after her, because he was frightened too.

And then a dreadful thing happened to my naughty little sister. That Bad Harry *stuck in the pipe* – and he couldn't get any farther. He was quite a round fat boy, you see, and he stuck fast as fast in the pipe.

Then didn't those sillies howl and howl!

My little sister howled because she didn't want to go on and on down the roadmen's pipes on her own, and Bad Harry howled because he couldn't move at all.

It was all terrible of course, but the roary workman rescued them very quickly. He couldn't reach Bad Harry with his arm, but he got a long hooky iron thing, and he hooked it in Bad Harry's belt, and he pulled and pulled, and presently he pulled Bad Harry out of the pipe. Wasn't it a good thing they had the hooky iron? And wasn't it a *very* good thing that Bad Harry had a strong belt on his coat?

When Bad Harry was out, my little sister wriggled back and back, and came out too, and when she saw all the poor workmen who wouldn't have any dinner, she cried and cried, and she told them what a sorry girl she was. She told the workmen that she and Bad Harry hadn't known the mackintoshy bundle was their dinners, and Bad Harry said he was sorry too, and they were so really truly ashamed that the big workman said, "Well, never mind this time. It's pay-day today, so we can send the boy for fish and chips instead," and he told my little sister not to cry any more.

So my little sister stopped crying, and she and Bad Harry both said they would never, never meddle and be inquisitive again.

27 · My naughty little sister and the solid silver watch

A LONG TIME ago, when I was a little girl and my naughty little sister was very small, we had a dear old grandfather. Our dear old grandfather lived very near to us, and sometimes he came to our house, and sometimes we went to visit him.

When our grandfather came to see us, he wore very beautiful black clothes and a very smart black hat, and my little sister would say, "Smart Grandad," because he looked so nice.

Our grandfather told my little sister that these smart clothes were his Sunday Blacks. He said he wore his Sunday Blacks when he went to church and when he went visiting, because they were his best clothes.

When our grandfather came to our house in his smart Sunday Blacks, he always sat down very carefully. He would put a big white handkerchief on his knees, and then lift my little sister up and let her sit on the big white handkerchief. But my little sister had to hold her legs out very carefully so that she wouldn't brush her dusty shoes on our grandfather's best Sunday Black trousers.

But when we went to see our grandfather in his house, he didn't wear his Sunday Blacks at all. He wore nice brown velvety trousers with straps under his knees, and a soft furry waistcoat. He had a lovely red and white handkerchief too, but he didn't put that on his knees for my little sister to sit on.

Oh no. Grandfather didn't mind my little sister's dirty shoes when he was wearing his velvety trousers. He would let her climb up on to his lap all on her own and didn't mind how dirty her shoes were.

When my little sister sat on grandfather's lap, she always rubbed her face against his waistcoat. If she rubbed her face against his Sunday Black waistcoat, she rubbed it very, very carefully. But when we were at grandfather's house she rubbed very hard against his soft furry one.

One day, when we were at our grandfather's house, and my naughty little sister was sitting in grandfather's lap, she said a funny thing, she said, "Grandad, I like your fur waistcoat better than your smart Sunday Black one. It smells tobacco-y. Your Sunday one smells mothball-y. I like tobacco better than mothball, I think."

Our grandfather laughed a lot and said he liked tobacco better than mothball too.

Then my little sister said, "Your Sunday waistcoat and your furry waistcoat both talk *nick-nock*, *nick-nock*. Why do they both talk *nick-nock*, Grandad?"

Our grandfather didn't know what she meant about *nick-nock*, so he looked at my little sister very hard. Then he smiled and said, "Of course, duckie, you mean my watch!"

Then our grandfather showed my little sister a thin leather strap that was on his waistcoat button and he said,

"Pull the strap and you'll see who it is that says *nick-nock* — it isn't my waistcoat that says it at all."

So my funny little sister pulled the thin leather strap. She pulled very slowly, and very carefully, because she was a little bit frightened, but when she had pulled enough out came a round silver box-thing with a round silver lid.

Our grandfather opened the round silver lid and there was a face just like the face on all the clocks everywhere.

"That's my watch," our grandfather told my little sister. "That is my solid silver watch. My old father had it once, and one day your father will have it. It is a very nice watch," our grandfather said, "it is *solid* silver."

My little sister held the solid silver watch very carefully and looked at its round white face and the black clock hands and the little round silver lid. Then my little sister put the solid silver watch against her ear and listened to it saying *nick-nock, nick-nock, nick-nock,* over and over again.

My little sister liked the watch so much that she held it all the time. Very carefully, like a good child, my little sister held the solid silver watch.

When it was time to go, our mother said, "You must give the watch back to Grandad now, so that he can put it in his pocket again," and my naughty little sister began to look cross, because she *did* like the solid silver watch so much.

But our grandfather said, "I will let you put him back to bed for me, duckie, then he will be quite safe until you see me again."

So then my little sister stopped being a cross girl and put the solid silver watch back into our grandfather's pocket her own self. She said, "I don't think I should like to go to bed in your pocket, Grandad. But the solid silver watch does. He still says *nick-nock*, doesn't he?"

After that my naughty little sister always asked to see the solid silver watch when she was with our grandfather, and he always let her hold it and listen to it say *nick-nock*.

And do you know, one evening, when our father and mother had to go out, our dear old grandfather came to look after us, and because my little sister was such a good girl, and went to bed so quietly, and said her prayers so nicely, our grandfather put his solid silver watch under her pillow, so that she could hear it say *nick-nock, nick-nock* until she fell asleep.

28 · The smart girl

ONE DAY THE Mayor of our town invited us to a children's garden party. Bad Harry was invited too, and so were all the other children who lived near us.

When Mrs Cocoa heard that my little sister was going to the Mayor's party she was very pleased because she loved my bad little sister very much, and so she made her a beautiful party-dress to wear.

Mrs Cocoa said that she had some nice material called Indian muslin in her drawer that would be just the thing for a party-dress.

The Indian muslin was all white with little white needlework flowers all over it. Mrs Cocoa made it into a dress for my little sister, and when it was finished she put a pink ribbon round the middle of it, and pink bows on the sleeves, and she made a frilly petticoat to go underneath it; and when my little sister tried it on she looked just like a beautiful new doll straight out of the box.

Bad Harry was there when my sister tried her dress on and he opened his eyes very wide.

"Nice," said Bad Harry. "You *do* look nice."

And he said, "Nice and nice and nice" to show my sister how very smart he thought she looked.

My little sister didn't say anything. She just stood on the table and looked at herself in the mirror over the

mantelpiece and was so very pleased she couldn't talk at all.

She was quite quiet until dear Mrs Cocoa said, "Don't you like it?" Then she spoke. She said, "Oh, Mrs Cocoa,

I am just like a fairy. I think I must take it off quickly before it gets dirty." That was a surprising thing for my little sister to say, for as a rule she didn't mind being dirty a bit.

When our mother had taken the dress off for her, my funny sister ran to Mrs Cocoa and hugged her and kissed her and said, "Dear Mrs Cocoa, I love my smart dress. I love it very much. I love me in it, too."

She wouldn't hug Mrs Cocoa while she had the dress on, because she was afraid of spoiling it. Wasn't she funny?

Before the party-day my little sister often went upstairs and asked our mother to let her peep into the wardrobe and see the Indian muslin dress, but she didn't want to try it on again; she wouldn't even touch it. She said she wanted it to be absolutely beautiful for the party. Wasn't she a strange child?

When the party-day came, and she saw me getting ready to go, my little sister said, "Mother, I will wear my smart dress *now*." And she stood straight and good on a chair while Mother washed her, and straight and good when she was dressed, and straight and good when her hair was brushed, because she wanted to look just like a fairy.

Bad Harry came to call for us. "Come on, come on," he said, because he was impatient, but my little sister would not hurry. She said "Good-bye" to our mother in a very quiet voice, and she took my hand like a good girl and walked along very neatly in her white shoes, not scuffling the dust or anything!

186

Mrs Cocoa came to her gate to see us off and my sister waved her hand to her. "I can't kiss you, Mrs Cocoa," she said, "because I am all neat and nice," and although Bad Harry said "Hurry! Hurry!" and ran ahead and back again and again she still walked very nicely and slowly with me.

At last we came to the Mayor's Garden Party place. It did look grand! The Mayor had hung lots of little coloured

flags all round his garden, and the big gates were open and a band was playing, and we could hear Punch-and-Judy noises and see stripy tents inside. Bad Harry was so excited that he just dashed ahead of us, and would have gone in on his own, if the gate man hadn't asked for his invitation card that I was carrying for him!

There were a lot of people crowding round the gate

watching the children going to the party, and one lady said, "Oh, the little duckie," when she saw my neat and nice sister, and my little sister felt very proud. But she didn't turn her head, and she didn't let go of my hand, because she wanted to look as fairy-like as possible!

The Mayor had made a lovely party for us. We soon found that the stripy tents had all sorts of interesting things in them. Things that you could do without paying for them. It was just like a lovely *free* fair!

There were hoop-la's and magic fish-ponds and swings and pony-rides and Mr Punch and a conjurer, all as free as free. There was even a coconut-shy, and we saw some of the bigger children throwing balls at the coconuts.

Wasn't it kind of the Mayor? We saw him walking in the garden with a gold chain round his neck, and he smiled at us and asked if we were having a good time. We said, "Yes, thank you," and he said, "Good. Good."

And we were enjoying ourselves. At least I was. And Bad Harry was. But my little sister didn't seem to be enjoying it very much at all. You see, she was afraid of spoiling her smart dress, and when the gentlemen with the round-abouts said, "Come on now, who wants a ride?" she couldn't say "Me! me!" because she wanted to look smart, and she was afraid she might get her dress dirty on the roundabouts; and when the fish-pond young lady said, "Come and fish for a magic prize," she said, "No, thank you, I might get wet!"

Bad Harry fished and he won a tin whistle, but, although she wanted a tin whistle very much, she wouldn't fish, oh no!

When we went to see Mr Punch she stood at the back of the crowd because of her sticking-out dress, and she was so far away that when Mr Punch smacked his baby, she didn't hear the nice man by the Punch show saying, "It's all right, children, he isn't really hurting it, you know!" and so of course she cried, and then she had to stop crying because she might make her Indian muslin dress all teary.

Bad Harry got quite cross at last and he said, "Why did you wear that silly old dress?"

My sister said, "It's not silly. It's smart."

And Harry said, "It's smart *and* it's silly if you can't do anything in it."

My little sister said, "I want to be smart."

Then Bad Harry said, "Well, if you keep on being smart like that you won't be able to have any of the Mayor's nice tea that the ladies are putting on the tables in that big tent over there. It's a very nice tea," Bad Harry said. "There are lots of cakes and jellies. I know because I've just been over there to look."

When my little sister heard about the tea and the jellies and when she thought about the roundabouts and the fish-pond she began to feel quite sorry. But she didn't want to spoil her smart dress.

189

She thought and thought. She saw the other children
running about and sliding on slides and eating ice-cream

and throwing balls at coconuts, and then she had a funny
idea.

Very, very quietly she walked away from the fair-place
and round behind some bushes where no one could see
her. I didn't notice her go, because Bad Harry and I were
trying to throw rings over some hooks on the hoop-la stall.

When I *did* find that she had gone, I was very worried,
especially as a big gentleman in a red coat began to bang
on a tray and call out, "Now, children, line up, and we
will go in to tea."

I must say I didn't want to have to go and look for my sister just at tea-time. I thought that the other children might eat all the cakes and jellies and things before I found her, and I wouldn't like that much.

But I *had* promised to look after her, so I began to ask people if they had seen her. I was just asking a lady, when I heard everyone burst out laughing.

All the boys and girls laughed, and the roundabout man, and the Punch man and the fish-pond lady, and the Mayor and Bad Harry. They laughed and laughed and laughed. They were laughing at my naughty little sister!

What do you think she had done?

She had got so tired of being careful of her beautiful dress that she had gone behind the bushes and *taken it off*! I don't know how she managed on her own – but she did.

She had taken off her dress and her lovely frilly petticoat and had put them very carefully over a garden seat, and out she jumped, her old noisy jumping self again, skipping up and down in her little white vest and her little white knickers! And she was laughing too.

"*Now* I can have swings, and fish-ponds, and round-abouts and a big tea," she shouted. "Now I can be *me* again." She was very pleased with her good idea.

"I shan't spoil my beautiful dress now," she said. "Aren't I a clever girl?"

What would you have said if she had been your Naughty Little Sister?

29 · The cross, spotty child

ONE DAY MY naughty little sister wasn't at all a well girl. She was all burny and tickly and tired and sad and spotty, and when our nice doctor came to see her he said, "You've got measles, old lady."

"You've got measles," that nice doctor said, "and you will have to stay in bed for a few days."

When my sister heard that she had measles she began to cry, "I don't want measles. Nasty measles," and made herself burnier and ticklier and sadder than ever.

Have you had measles? Have you? If you have you will remember how nasty it is. I am sure that if you did have measles at any time you would be a very good child. You wouldn't fuss and fuss. But my sister did, I'm sorry to say.

She fidgeted and fidgeted and fussed and cried and had to be read to all the time, and wouldn't drink her orange-juice and lost her hanky in the bed until our mother said, "Oh dear, I don't want you to have measles, I'm sure."

She *was* a cross, spotty child.

When our mother had to go out to do her shopping, kind Mrs Cocoa Jones came in to sit with my sister. Mrs

Cocoa brought her knitting with her, and sat by my sister's bed and knitted and knitted. Mrs Cocoa was a kind lady and when my little sister moaned and grumbled she said,

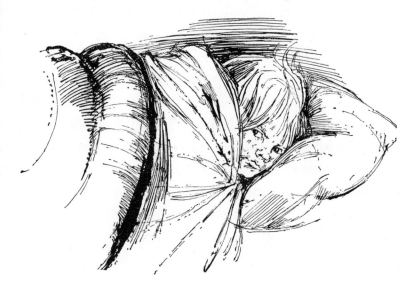

"There, there, duckie," in a very kind way.

My little sister didn't like Mrs Cocoa saying "There, there, duckie" to her, because she was feeling cross herself, so she pulled the sheet over her face and said, "Go away, Mrs Cocoa."

But Mrs Cocoa didn't go away; she just went on knitting and knitting until my naughty little sister pulled the sheet down from her face to see what Mrs Cocoa could be doing and whether she had made her cross.

But kind Mrs Cocoa wasn't cross – she was just sorry to see my poor spotty sister, and when she saw my sister looking at her, she said, "Now, I was just thinking. I believe I have the very thing to cheer you up."

My sister was surprised when Mrs Cocoa said this instead of being cross with her for saying "Go away" so she listened hard and forgot to be miserable.

"When I was a little girl," Mrs Cocoa said, "my granny didn't like to see poor not-well children looking miserable, so she made a get-better box that she used to lend to all her grandchildren when they were ill."

Mrs Cocoa said, "My granny kept this box on top of her dresser, and when she found anything that she thought might amuse a not-well child she would put it in her box."

Mrs Cocoa said that it was a great treat to borrow the get-better box because although you knew some of the things that would be in it, there was always something fresh.

My little sister stopped being cross and moany while she listened to Mrs Cocoa, because she hadn't heard of a get-better box before.

She said, "What things, Mrs Cocoa? What was in the box?"

"All kinds of things," Mrs Cocoa said.

"Tell me! Tell me!" said my spotty little sister and she began to look cross because she wanted to know so much.

But Mrs Cocoa said, "I won't tell you, for you can see for yourself."

Mrs Cocoa said, "I hadn't thought about it until just

this very minute; but do you know, I've got my granny's very own get-better box in my house and I had forgotten all about it! It's up in an old trunk in the spare bedroom. There are a lot of heavy boxes on top of the trunk, but if you are a good girl now, I will ask Mr Cocoa to get them down for me when he comes home from work. I will get the box out of the trunk and bring it in for you to see tomorrow."

Wasn't that a beautiful idea?

Mrs Cocoa Jones said, "I haven't seen that box for years and years, it will be quite a treat to look in it again. I am sure it will be just the thing to lend to a cross little spotty girl with measles, don't you?"

And my naughty little sister thought it *was* just the thing indeed!

So, next morning, as soon as my sister had had some bread and milk and a spoonful of medicine, Mrs Cocoa came upstairs to see her, with her grandmother's get-better box under her arm.

There was a *smiling* spotty child waiting for her today.

It was a beautiful-looking box, because Mrs Cocoa's old grandmother had stuck beautiful pieces of wallpaper on the lid and on the sides of the box, and Mrs Cocoa said that the wallpaper on the front was some that had been in her granny's front bedroom, and that on the back had been in her parlour. The paper on the lid had come from her Aunty Kitty's sitting-room; the paper on one side had

been in Mrs Cocoa's mother's kitchen, while the paper on
the other side which was really lovely, with roses and
green dickeybirds, had come from Mrs Cocoa's own bedroom wallpaper when she was a little girl!

My sister was so interested to hear this that she almost
forgot about opening the box!

But she did open it, and she found so many things that
I can only tell you about some of them.

On top of the box she found a lovely piece of shining
stuff folded very tidily, and when she opened it out on her
bed she saw that it was covered with round sparkly things
that Mrs Cocoa said were called spangles. Mrs Cocoa
said that it was part of a dress that a real fairy queen had
worn in a real pantomime. She said that a lady who had
worked in a theatre had given it to her grandmother long,
long ago.

Under the sparkly stuff were boxes and boxes. Tiny boxes with pretty pictures painted on the lids, and in every box a nice little interesting thing. A string of tiny beads, or a little-little dollie, or some shells. In one box was a very little paper fan, and in another there was a little laughing clown's face cut out of paper that Mrs Cocoa's granny had stuck there as a surprise.

My sister was so surprised that she smiled, and Mrs Cocoa told her that her granny had put that in to make a not-well child be surprised and smile. She said that she remembered smiling at that box when she was a little girl.

Mrs Cocoa's old granny had been very clever, hadn't she?

There were picture postcards in that not-well box, and pretty stones – some sparkly and some with holes in them. There was a small hard fir cone, and pieces of coloured glass that you could hold up before your eyes and look through. There was a silver pencil with a hole in the handle that you could look through too and see a magic picture.

There was a small book with pictures in it – oh, I can't remember what else!

It amused and amused my sister.

She took all the things out carefully and then she put them all back carefully. She shut the lid and looked at the wallpaper outside all over again.

Then she took the things out again, and looked at them

197

again and played with them and was as interested as could be!

And Mrs Cocoa said, "Well, I never! That's just what I did myself when I was a child!"

When my sister was better she gave the box back to Mrs Cocoa – just as Mrs Cocoa had given the box back to her granny.

Mrs Cocoa Jones laid all the things from the box out in the sunshine in her back garden to air them after the measles. She said her grandmother always did that, and because Mrs Cocoa's granny had done it, it made it all very specially nice for my little sister to think about.

After that, my sister often played at making a get-better box with a boot-box that Mother gave her, and once she drew red chalk spots on poor Rosy-primrose's face so that she could have measles and the get-better box to play with.

30 · What a jealous child!

MY NAUGHTY LITTLE sister had a godmother-auntie whom she loved very much.

This godmother-auntie was a very, very kind, and very, very pretty young lady. My little sister used to say that she was like a fairy in a book. She had curly gold hair and twinkling blue eyes and she was always laughing and singing.

And she was never cross. She used to have a lovely hat with cherries on it, and one day my greedy sister pulled the cherries off her hat and tried to eat them, and she didn't grumble at all. When she saw the dreadful face my naughty little sister was making when she found that those hat-cherries were full of nasty cottonwool stuff she only laughed, and said, "If you'd *told* me you wanted them to play with you could have had them, and then I would have explained that they were not real."

And when our mother scolded my sister this pretty lady said, "Don't worry, I was going to put a rose on that hat anyway."

And the next time she came to see us she *had* put a rose

on her hat – a big pink one, and to please my little sister she had brought along a small pink rose for her to wear on *her* hat! "Only don't try to eat that," she said, "because it is made of silk and won't taste at all nice."

Wasn't she kind?

This beautiful godmother worked in a big sweetie shop in London where they made specially grand sweeties in a big kitchen behind the shop, and she used to tell my sister and me all about how the sweeties were made.

She told us how the sweeties were rolled in sugar and cut with real silver knives, and how all the fruity pieces in them came right across the sea from France in wooden boxes, and we were very interested.

She always brought us a big box of sweeties from her shop and they were grander than any sweeties we'd ever seen before. They were in a very smart silky box with

flowers on it, and the box was tied up with real hair-ribbony ribbon that our mother always put away in her ribbon box.

When our mother saw the beautiful tied-up box she always said, "It looks too pretty to open." But we *did* open it.

And when the box was opened she would say, "They look too nice to eat." But we *did* eat them, and Mother always had the first one – and she always took the almondy one in the middle with the green bits sticking out of it, because there was only one of those, and she didn't want my sister and me to be cross about who should have it.

My little sister loved those boxes of sweeties because her godmother-aunt had told her all about the big shop and the place where they were made, and she would be very careful before she chose her sweet, and when she did choose it she would say, "Tell me about this one, godma-aunt."

And she would hear all over again about silver knives and French cherries and men in white caps who twisted the sweetie stuff on hooks and pulled it out and p-u-l-l-e-d it out to make it clear and shiny.

When her beautiful godmother said, "Pulled it out" she would make pulling-out faces and speak in a pulling-out voice.

She would say, "P-u-l-l-e-d i-t o-u-t" – like that.

How my sister would laugh. She always wanted to hear

about the pulling out of the sweetie stuff when her god-mother came to see us.

We were always glad to see my little sister's godmother, she was so very nice. My little sister liked seeing her best of all. She liked to climb on to her godmother's lap and

stare at her pretty smily face. She would pat her cheeks and say, "Sing to me, godma-aunt. Sing me a funny song."

And her godmother would sing her all sorts of funny songs until my sister's eyes got all peepy and teary with laughing so much.

Then my sister, who was not a kissing child at all, would

hug and kiss her pretty godmother-auntie and say, "I do love you, you nice lady!"

Wasn't she a lovely godmother to have?

Now, you wouldn't think that anyone could ever be cross with such a dear lady, would you?

You would be surprised to hear that someone shouted at her and said, "Go away, I don't want you," wouldn't you?

I know I was surprised when my sister behaved like that to her dear godmother. But she did. And do you know why? It's because she was an unpleasant, jealous girl.

You see, one day her dear godmother brought a great tall man to see us. She had never brought anyone else before, and my sister didn't quite like it. She liked to have her godmother on her own. She said, "I'm shy," and ran and hid her face in Mother's lap, and when Mother told her to sit on a chair and to stop being silly, she sat and stared at her godmother-aunt and the great tall man and looked cross as cross.

Do you know why she behaved like that?

It was because the great tall man liked her godmother-aunt too, and it was because her godmother-aunt liked the tall man very much.

My naughty little sister didn't want her godmother to like anyone but her, and she didn't want the big tall man to like her godmother.

She was jealous. And that is a very nasty thing to be,

isn't it? What a good thing you aren't a child like that.

My sister pretended that she didn't want any sweeties, and her poor godmother looked quite worried.

"But Albert made some of them," she said.

Albert was the great tall man.

Our grandmother started to tell us all about Albert making the sweeties, but my sister wouldn't listen. She got down from her chair and said, "I want to go to bed now."

Do you know that was in the morning, and she hadn't had her dinner. Wasn't she being awkward?

Mother said, "You behave yourself, you naughty little girl."

But the beautiful godmother-auntie said, "Don't be cross with her; I think she's not sure about Albert."

She smiled very kindly at my sister and said, "You must like Albert, duckie. Albert and I are going to get married very soon and we shall be living in a dear little house and you can come and stay with us." And she came over to my sister in a kind way.

When my sister heard this, when she heard that the great tall man and her pretty godmother-aunt were going to be married, she was so cross that she said what I told you.

She said, "Go away. I don't want you."

She said, "I don't want you and I don't want that great tall man. You can go away now."

Oh dear! Our mother was cross! But what do you think? That great big tall Albert man started to laugh, and he had such a loud roary laugh that my sister forgot to be jealous and stared at him.

When Albert laughed my sister's godmother began to laugh too, and they made so much noise that our mother began to laugh as well, and so did I – you never heard so much laughing.

Then that funny Albert man got up and opened a big

bag that he had brought with him, and he took out a big, wide saucepan. Then he took out a bag of sugar and some butter and some treacle stuff in a tin. He was laughing all the time he did it because my sister was staring so much!

He took these things to our mother's kitchen and he began to cook all the sugar and stuff in his saucepan. He didn't say anything, he just cooked.

No one had ever done a thing like that in our house before, so my sister went on being not jealous, and went out into the kitchen to see what he was doing instead.

When Albert saw my sister looking at him he put his hand into his bag and took out a white hat and put it on his head.

And he cooked and cooked and stirred with a spoon and cooked until all the sugar-butter-treacly stuff began to smell very nice indeed.

Then Albert took the saucepan off the stove, and did another funny thing.

He took the towel off the hook behind our kitchen door, and he wiped the hook very clean with our mother's dish-cloth and dried it beautifully on the tea-towel.

My sister's eyes said "O" "O", she was so astonished.

Then, all of a sudden, Albert took the warm sticky stuff out of the saucepan and threw it over the hook.

Then he got a hold on the end of it and he p-u-l-l-e-d it and he p-u-l-l-e-d it. Then he twisted it up and he threw it back over the hook and he p-u-l-l-e-d and p-u-l-l-e-d it again, quick as quick.

It was just like my sister's godmother had told us. And it wasn't in the shop-kitchen either, it was in our own mother's own kitchen.

Albert pulled that stuff until it was clear and then he took it off the hook, quick as quick! It was all long and twisty.

It was a beautiful thing to do, wasn't it?

Albert didn't speak to my sister, he just spoke out loud to himself; he said, "I wonder if it tastes all right?"

He got a hammer and began to break the long twisty piece of toffee-stuff. When he did this, a piece jumped right off the table and fell by my sister's foot.

Our kitchen smelled so nice and the sweetie looked so nice, that my sister picked that piece up and popped it into her mouth and it was quite delicious.

Now she wasn't jealous at all. She was proud. She was proud to think that she knew such a clever man. "It is very, very nice, Albert," she said. "You are very clever."

Then she laughed and Albert laughed, and Albert let her put his funny white cap on, and her godmother lifted her up so that she could see herself in the glass wearing the white cap, and everyone was very happy.

My sister looked at her lovely smiling godmother and the great, tall, clever Albert and she said, "I don't mind Albert being my godmother-uncle after all."

3I · My naughty little sister makes a bottle-tree

MY NAUGHTY LITTLE sister got up very early one morning, and while my mother was cooking the breakfast, my naughty little sister went quietly, quietly out of the kitchen door, and quietly, quietly up the garden-path. Do you know why she went quietly like that? It was because she was up to mischief.

She didn't stop to look at the flowers, or the marrows or the runner-beans, and she didn't put her fingers in the water-tub. No! She went right along to the tool-shed to find a trowel. You know what trowels are, of course, but my naughty little sister didn't. She called a trowel "a digger".

"Where is the digger?" said my naughty little sister to herself.

Well, she found the trowel, and she took it down the garden until she came to a very nice place in the big flower-bed. Then she stopped and began to dig and dig with the trowel, which you know was a most naughty thing to do, because of all the little baby seeds that are waiting to come up in flower-beds sometimes.

Shall I tell you why my naughty little sister dug that hole? All right, I will. It was because she wanted to plant a brown, shiny acorn. So, when she had made a really nice deep hole, she put the acorn in it, and covered it all up again with earth, until the brown, shiny acorn was all gone.

Then my naughty little sister got a stone, and a leaf, and a stick, and she put them on top of the hole, so that she could remember where the acorn was, and then she went indoors to have her hands washed for breakfast. She didn't tell me, or my mother or anyone about the acorn. She kept it for her secret.

Well now, my naughty little sister kept going down the garden all that day, to look at the stone, the leaf and the stick, on top of her acorn-hole, and my naughty little sister smiled and smiled to herself because she knew that there was a brown, shiny acorn under the earth.

But when my father came home, he was very cross. He said, "Who's been digging in my flower-bed?"

And my little sister said, "I have."

Then my father said, "You are a bad child. You've disturbed all the little baby seeds!"

And my naughty little sister said, "I don't care about the little baby seeds, I want a home for my brown, shiny acorn."

So my father said, "Well, *I* care about the little baby seeds myself, so I shall dig your acorn up for you, and you must find another home for it," and he dug it up for her at once, and my naughty little sister tried all over the garden to find a new place for her acorn.

But there were beans and marrows and potatoes and lettuce and tomatoes and roses and spinach and radishes, and no room at all for the acorn, so my naughty little sister grew crosser and crosser and when tea-time came she wouldn't eat her tea. Aren't you glad you don't show off like that?

Then my mother said, "Now don't be miserable. Eat up your tea and you shall help me to plant your acorn in a bottleful of water."

So my naughty little sister ate her tea after all, and then my mother, who was a clever woman, filled a bottle with water, and showed my naughty little sister how to put the acorn in the top of the bottle. Shall I tell you how she did it, in case you want to try?

Well now, my naughty little sister put the pointy end of the acorn into the water, and left the bottom of the acorn sticking out of the top – (the bottom end, you know, is the end that sits in the little cup when it's on the tree).

"Now," said my mother, "you can watch its little root grow in the water."

My naughty little sister had to put her acorn in lots of bottles of water, because the bottles were always getting broken, as she put them in such funny places. She put them on the kitchen window-sill where the cat walked, and on the side of the bath, and inside the bookcase, until my mother said, "We'll put it on top of the cupboard, and I will get it down for you to see every morning after breakfast."

Then, at last, the little root began to grow. It pushed down, down into the bottle of water and it made lots of other little roots that looked just like whitey fingers, and my little sister was pleased as pleased. Then, one day, a little shoot came out of the top of the acorn, and broke all the browny outside off, and on this little shoot were two little baby leaves, and the baby leaves grew and grew, and my mother said, "That little shoot will be a big tree one day."

My naughty little sister was very pleased. When she was pleased she danced and danced, so you can just guess how she danced to think of her acorn growing into a tree.

"Oh," she said, "when it's a tree we can put a swing on it, and I can swing indoors on my very own tree."

But my mother said, "Oh, no. I'm afraid it won't like being indoors very much now; it will want to grow out under the sky."

Then my little sister had a good idea. And now, this is a *good thing* about my little sister – she had a very kind thought about her little tree. She said, "I know! When we go for a walk we'll take my bottle-tree and the digger (which, of course, you call a trowel) and we will plant it in the park, just where there are no trees, so it can grow and grow and spread and spread into a big tree."

And that is just what she did do. Carefully, carefully, she took her bottle-tree out of the bottle, and put it in her little basket, and then we all went out to the park. And when my little sister had found a good place for her little bottle-tree, she dug a nice deep hole for it, and then she put her tree into the hole, and gently, gently put the earth all round its roots, until only the leaves and stem were showing, and when she'd planted it in, my mother showed her how to pat the earth with the trowel.

Then at last the little tree was in the kind of place it really liked, and my little sister had planted it all by herself.

Now you will be pleased to hear that the little bottle-tree grew and grew and now it's quite a big tree. Taller than my naughty little sister, and she's quite a big lady nowadays.

32 · My naughty little sister
goes to the Pantomime

A LONG TIME ago, when I was a little girl, and my little sister was a little girl too, my mother took us to see the Christmas Pantomime.

The Pantomime was in a theatre, which was a very beautiful place with red tippy-up seats and a lot of ladies and gentlemen playing music in front of the curtains.

My little sister was a very good quiet child at first, because she had never been to the Pantomime before. She sat very still and mousy. She didn't say anything. She just looked and looked.

She looked at the lights, and the lots and lots of seats, and the music-people and the other boys and girls. She didn't even fidget at first, because she wasn't quite sure about the tippy-up seat.

When we were in the theatre, our mother gave us a bag of sweets each. I had chocolate-creams, and my little sister had toffee-drops, because she liked them so much, but she was so quiet that she didn't eat even a single one of them before the Pantomime started.

She just held the sweeties on her lap, so that when the
music man who plays the cymbals suddenly made them
go "Rish-tish a-tish!" and the curtains came back, she
was so surprised that she dropped them all over the floor,
and my mother had to pick them up for her.

My little sister was so surprised because she hadn't
known that Pantomime was people dancing and singing
and falling over things, but when she saw that it was, she
was very excited, and when the other children clapped
their hands, she clapped hers very hard too.

At first, my little sister was so surprised that she liked every bit of it, but after a while she said her favourite was the fat funny man. The play was all about the Babes in the Wood, and the fat funny man was called Humpty Dumpty. He was very very funny indeed, and when he came on, he always said, "Hallo, boys and girls."

And the boys and girls said, "Hallo, Humpty Dumpty."

And he said, "How are you tomorrow?" and we said, "We are very well today." He told us to say this every time, and we never forgot. Once, my little sister shouted so loud, "Hallo, Humpty Dumpty," she shouted "Hallo, Humpty Dumpty", like that, that Humpty Dumpty heard her, and he waved specially to her. My goodness, wasn't she a proud girl then!

The other thing my little sister liked was the fairies

dancing. There were lots of fairies in the Pantomime, and they had lovely sparkly dresses, and when they danced the lights went red and blue and green, and some of them really flew right up in the air!

Humpty Dumpty tried to fly too, but he fell right over and bumped his nose. My naughty little sister was so sorry for him, that she began to cry and cry, really true tear-crying, not just howling.

But when Humpty Dumpty jumped up and said, "Hallo, boys and girls," and we all said, "Hello, Humpty Dumpty," and when he began to dance again, she knew he wasn't really hurt so she laughed and laughed.

And presently, what do you think? My little sister had a really exciting thing happen.

Humpty Dumpty came on the stage and he sang a little song for all the boys and girls, and then he made all the children sing too. After that he said, "Will any little boy or girl like to come up on the stage and dance with me?" And do you know what, my little sister said, "Yes. I will. I will." And she ran out of her seat and up the stage steps and right on to the big theatre stage before my mother could do anything about it.

All the people cheered and clapped when my little sister ran up on to the stage, and a lot of other boys and girls went up too then, and soon they were all dancing with Humpty Dumpty. Round and round and up and down, until two ladies dressed like men came on the stage.

Then Humpty Dumpty said, "All right, children, down you go," and all the boys and girls went down again, off the stage and back to their mothers.

All except my bad little sister. *Because she wasn't there.* She'd vanished! And what do you think?

While the two ladies dressed like men were singing on the stage, the funny man came back, with my little sister sitting on his shoulder. And he came right off the stage and down the steps and brought her back to Mother, and my little sister looked very pleased and smily.

All the people stared and stared to see my naughty little sister being carried back by Humpty Dumpty. Even the singing ladies dressed like men stared.

And do you know where she had been?

The bad child had slipped round the side of the stage while the other children were dancing, to see if she could find the fairies!

And she did find them too. She said they were drinking lemonade and they gave her some as well. It wasn't very fairyish lemonade, she said, it was the fizzy nose-tickle sort.

She told us another thing too, a secret thing. She said they weren't real true fairies, only little girls like herself, and she said that when she was a bit older, she was going to be a stage fairy like those little girls.

33 · The wiggly tooth

WHEN I WAS a little girl, and my naughty little sister was a very little girl, we used to have an apple-tree in our garden, and sometimes my naughty little sister used to pick the apples and eat them. It was a very easy thing to do because the branches were so low.

So, my mother told us we were not to pick the apples. My mother said, "It is naughty to pick the apples when they are growing upon the tree, because we want them to go on growing until they are ripe and rosy, and then we shall pick them and put them away for the winter-time."

"If you want an apple," my mother said, "you must pick up a windfall and bring it to me, and I will wash it for you."

As you know, "windfalls" are apples that fall off the tree on to the grass, so, one day, my little sister looked under the tree and found a nice big windfall on the grass, and she took it in for my mother to wash.

When my mother had washed the apple, *and* cut out the specky bit where the little maggot had gone to live, my little sister sat down on the step to eat her big apple.

She opened her mouth very wide, because it *was* such a big apple, and she took a big bite. And what do you think happened? She felt a funny cracky sort of feeling in her mouth. My naughty little sister was so surprised that she nearly tumbled off the step when she felt the funny cracky feeling in her mouth, and she put in her finger to see what the crackiness was, and she found that one of her nice little teeth was loose.

So my naughty little sister ran indoors to my mother, and she said, "Oh, dear, my tooth has gone all loose and wiggly, what shall I do?" in a waily whiny voice because at first she didn't like it very much.

My mother said, "There's nothing to worry about. All your nice little baby-teeth will come out one by one to make room for your big grown-up teeth."

"Have a look, have a look," said my naughty little sister. So my mother had a look, and then she said, "It's just as I thought, there is a new little tooth peeping through already."

So after that my little sister had a loose tooth, and she used to wiggle it and wiggle it with her finger. She used to wiggle it so much that the tooth got looser and looser.

When the nice baker came, my naughty little sister showed him the tooth, and she showed the milkman and the window-cleaner man, and sometimes she used to climb up to the mirror and wiggle it hard, to show herself,

because she thought that a loose tooth was a very special thing to have.

After a while, my mother said, "Your tooth is so very loose, you had better let me take it out for you."

But my naughty little sister didn't want to lose her lovely tooth, because she liked wiggling it so much, and she wouldn't let my mother take it out at all.

Then my mother said, "Well, pull it out yourself, then," and my silly little sister said, "No, I like it like this."

The next time the window-cleaner man came, he said, "Isn't that toothy-peg out yet?"

And my naughty little sister said, "No. It's still here." And she opened her mouth very wide to show the window-cleaner man that it was still there.

The window-cleaner man said, "Why don't you pull it out? It's hanging on a threddle, it is indeed."

My naughty little sister told him that she liked to have it to wiggle and to show people.

So the window-cleaner man said, "You'd better take it to show the dentist."

My naughty little sister said why should she take it to the dentist? Because she hadn't heard much about dentists, and the window-cleaner man who knew all about doctors and dentists and about how the sun moves and how pumpkins grow, told my naughty little sister all about dentists, how they looked after people's teeth for them, and made teeth for grown-up people who hadn't any of their own.

The window-cleaner man told my naughty little sister that *his* teeth were dentist-teeth and they were much prettier than his old ones, and my naughty little sister was very interested, and she said she would like the dentist to see her wiggly tooth.

So, the next time my mother said, "What about that tooth, now?" My naughty little sister said, "I want to go to the dentist."

My mother said, "Goodness me, surely it's loose enough for you to pull out yourself now?"

But my naughty little sister started to cry, "I want to go to the dentist. I want to go, I do." In a miserable voice like that.

So my mother said, "Very well then. I want the dentist